BLACK

BEAR

CREEK

stories

JOSHUA
CROSS

BLACK BEAR CREEK

stories

JOSHUA CROSS

SOUTHEAST MISSOURI STATE UNIVERSITY PRESS | 2021

BLACK BEAR CREEK BY JOSHUA CROSS

COPYRIGHT 2021: JOSHUA CROSS

ISBN: 978-1-7330153-1-8
SOFTCOVER: $18.00

FIRST PUBLISHED IN 2021 BY
SOUTHEAST MISSOURI STATE UNIVERSITY PRESS
ONE UNIVERSITY PLAZA, MS 2650
CAPE GIRARDEAU, MO 63701
WWW.SEMOPRESS.COM

Library of Congress Cataloging-in-Publication Data
Names: Cross, Joshua, author.
Title: Black Bear Creek: stories / Joshua Cross.
Description: Cape Girardeau, MO : Southeast Missouri State University, 2021.
Identifiers: LCCN 2020040746 | ISBN 9781733015318 (paperback)
Subjects: LCGFT: Short stories.
Classification: LCC PS3603.R6746 B57 2021 | DDC 813/.6--dc23
LC record available at https://lccn.loc.gov/2020040746

FOR JESS AND CALLUM

CONTENTS

DESSERT IN THE DINNER HOLE

WHEN I DROPPED OUT OF COLLEGE, THE FACT I WOULD GO TO WORK in the mines was almost predetermined, but for a few years I resisted. I took a job in a full-service gas station. Between customers I sat in the cramped and humid glass booth in the middle of the asphalt and rows of pumps, and I read Milan Kundera and listened to NPR, surrounded by racks of snack cakes and chips and cigarettes. Shit work, but it paid enough to afford rent and cable and an occasional dimebag. But then Ami got pregnant and she wouldn't agree to take care of it even though I offered to pay for the procedure. She was raised Catholic, so she's got hang-ups. Her parents threatened to disown her, so we had a white wedding before she got fat, and I went to work for International Coal Group to support my new family.

The fucked-up part? She miscarried a few months after I started working for ICG. I considered asking if this meant the marriage was annulled but decided against it.

ICG opened a new mine in Eccles, a tiny shithole outside Beckley, the larger shithole where I was raised and where Ami and I met and started our shotgun lives. By the time I applied, the mine was staffed and we thought I would have to seek work elsewhere. When a spot opened, I took their training classes and learned precautions against the dangers every child reared in the coalfields knows by heart: black lung and hearing loss and mine explosions and all those terrors you find deep in the earth.

My first night—I started on graveyard, working from the middle of the night to daybreak, though night and day vary little when you're buried alive—I changed in the shower house and heard the older miners joking and rough-housing. I tried not to act nervous, and at first they ignored me. We gathered in front of the shaft and soon the elevator opened and we packed into the cage and started down into darkness. I realized I forgot to flip on my cap light. When it lit, a gruff voice in front of me demanded I get that goddamn light out of his eyes. I looked at my toes and hoped he would take this gesture as apology—most of these men were larger than me, harder, and they knew I wasn't one of them yet because I wore the red hat of a trainee.

I could see nothing until the cage doors opened and the men in front of me moved into the black tunnel. The rock glistened and my light reflected black when I moved my head around the walls. White dust covered everything, rock dust to keep the coal dust down, to keep it from blowing you and hundreds of others to bejesus.

The entry tunnel extended into the mountain, a long shaft carved into the rock that seemed to stretch on forever. Every eighty feet, rooms were cut on both sides where the coal had been mined away. I followed the men deeper into the entry, trying my damnedest not to trip on the rough floor or over my feet in the steel-plated boots that were heavier than anything I'd ever worn, but my toe caught on a crag and I fell. Several of the men laughed when they turned back and saw me on my hands and knees.

"You Collison?" one of them said, stepping forward. I looked up at this man with a white beard stained yellow around the mouth. He was a head taller than me and probably twice my weight, and he winced at my cap light in his face. I looked away, told myself to never look a man in the face as long it could be helped.

"Name's Aaron," he said but didn't raise a hand to shake. His hands looked large enough to fit both my fists inside one palm. "Put your pail in the dinner hole and follow me." He pointed to one of the rooms where pails and thermoses circled the black walls.

I remembered my father coming home covered in coal dust, his round-topped metal lunchbox and his olive-drab thermos both coated in black, and I'd tried to buy a pail and thermos like his. When I was small I would step into his boots, which came to my hips, and try to walk until he told me to stop scuffing the floor. He left us when I was eight, before he ever taught me the things I would need to know down here.

"Your job," Aaron said, "is to follow and listen and do what I tell you until you get your black hat."

"How long will that take?"

"Depends on how well you listen."

He led me to a low trailer hooked to what looked like a tractor, both of them painted bus yellow and smeared in black like all the equipment I would see in the mine. We started loading supplies that we would drive to the face and set up for the day shift. As a supply man, this was the extent of my job.

I sweated as we loaded the trailer. You have to dress warm to keep off the chill of the mine, but the clothes are too warm for the labor, so you sweat constantly. When we climbed on the open tractor, what Aaron called the "man ride," and drove the supplies to the face, wind from the large ventilation fans blew back against us, and the farther we went the colder I got until I was shivering. When we unloaded the supplies at the face I began to sweat again. Every trip back and forth, I hated the man ride more.

The rest of the night I loaded and hauled every supply the day shift needed—bags of rock dust and long steel roof bolts, wooden roof beams and stone blocks called stopping, drums of oil and grease for the machines, tools of every ilk. The work was beneath me, I thought. Load the shit, drive to the face. Unload the shit, drive back. Repeat. And repeat and repeat.

Aaron wasn't much of a talker. Conversation was difficult in the first place. The noise of machines echoed throughout the mine, so only shouts carried through, and we had to wear dosimeters to measure our noise exposure. When we did speak, our conversation was brief and one-sided: Aaron gave me commands, and I followed them and cursed under my breath.

The other men didn't talk to me either.

Our work was hard, but the night went fast. Lunchtime came and everyone acted happy. We went to the dinner hole and claimed our supplies and dug into them, most of the men forming small groups, reminding me of my high school cafeteria, the loudest and most raucous forming a large group in the middle, the Black guys off to themselves in one clique on the perimeter.

I ate with Aaron, and he described the lunch pail his grandfather carried in the mines, a large circular bucket divided into three sections—the bottom for water, the middle for lunch, the top for dessert. "Wide enough to hold a whole pie," he said.

Aaron rooted in his pail, his hand passing the bagged sandwich and apple to find the plastic-wrapped snack cake. "Granddaddy always said eat dessert first," he told me, tearing the wrapper. "You never know when you might die down here."

*

AFTER LUNCH WE WENT BACK TO WORK AND SWEATED AND LOADED and hauled and soon quitting time came and the men were happier and rowdier than at lunchtime. We rode the elevator and they laughed and joked. I stood with Aaron toward the back, neither of us taking part. I was too tired to laugh, thinking only of sleep, my body aching. At the top, the cage opened onto frosted grass and a gray sunrise over the ridge beyond. The dayshift miners stood around the outside of the shaft, none of them laughing. They greeted some of our crew as we disembarked and they boarded the elevator behind us and the cage slid shut and they disappeared into the earth.

We filed toward the shower house. Once inside the building, I undressed and left my clean clothes on a bench in the locker room. When I entered the large open shower with dozens of nozzles, a man washing under each one and several other guys lined around them, I saw metal baskets suspended from the ceiling, all full of clothes the men had placed inside before pulling the baskets up away from the water. Rather than shampoo, we had large bottles of liquid dish soap to wash both hair and body, which cleared off most of the dust but left me feeling grimy.

I was one of the last to shower and when I came out, most of the men had driven away in their pickups and SUVs. My clothes weren't on the bench. I stood there naked, dripping, looking all over the room for where they'd thrown my neatly folded stack of clothes. When I'd searched everywhere inside, I looked out the window and saw knots of fabric piled atop a picnic table.

I ran into the freezing morning buck-ass naked and barefoot, feeling like one of those polar bear club idiots who dive into arctic lakes. I grabbed my clothes and ran back to the shower house, cat-calls pealing from men behind me.

Once I unknotted my clothes and pulled them on and walked back outside, I found Aaron smoking with a group of men. They laughed and whistled at me, all of them but Aaron. I started to my car, and he followed.

"Guess you learned not to leave your clothes on the bench," he said.

*

THAT FIRST NIGHT, I CAME HOME AT DAWN AND KICKED OFF THE boots outside the back door, walked in, and stripped on my way to the bedroom. I slid into bed beside Ami. The covers were pulled tight around her and she slept on her back, so I could see the faint pooch of her belly and the large mounds of her breasts. My body ached from the work and my mind ached for sleep, but I grew hard looking at her shape beneath the comforter. I scooted against her, pressing my erection into her outer thigh, and I took her earlobe between my teeth.

My relationship with Ami was purely physical from the beginning. She was never the type of person I thought I'd marry, not the type of girl you bring home to meet the extended family. She seemed the type of girl you meet in a bar and don't call after. Except when I met her, she wasn't old enough to pick up in a bar. I turned twenty-one the fall before, and she was just seventeen. We bought pot from the same guy behind the bleachers at the middle school, and one day we met and I invited her into my car to get stoned. Six months later she was pregnant.

When I pressed my body against her that night after work, she stirred and pushed against me, rolling away from me onto her side. I put my erection between her legs.

"Stop," she said. "Go back to sleep."

"I just got home," I said. "From work."

She mumbled and rolled to her side facing me and pushed against my chest to try to scoot me to the other side of the bed.

"Please baby," I said.

"You smell like dish soap," she said.

I knew I wouldn't get anywhere so I went to the bathroom and did it myself. When I came back to bed, she was asleep on her belly.

*

THE PRANKS AT WORK DIDN'T END WITH THE FIRST NIGHT'S MISSING clothing. One morning while I showered, some clever joker nailed my boots to the floor in the exact spot I'd left them standing. I learned to put my clothes in the baskets hanging from the ceiling, but I made the mistake of not hoisting the heavy boots with them. When I lowered my basket and pulled on the fresh clothes, I returned to the locker where I stored my work clothes and slid my feet into the boots and tried to walk but couldn't lift my legs. At first I felt like a child again, trying to move my father's boots. But I realized the situation for what it was and had to search the shop for a hammer to pry out the nails, and I scraped a bare foot on some antique and rusted auger lying on the floor.

Another favorite was I'd be talking to one guy and another would run up behind me, lift my shirt, and rub a handful of grease on my back. They did this every chance they got. I learned to stand with my back to a wall or a machine at all times—having equipment like the Continuous Miner running behind you isn't the best safety practice, but I figured the risk of death was slimmer than the risk of being greased by some asshole.

The prank that ticked me off most was the time someone took my bottle of dish soap, emptied and rinsed it out, and filled it with hydraulic fluid. I didn't notice until I poured the stuff over my head and body and began to lather. I smelled what I knew wasn't soap. Trying to rinse off the hydraulic fluid was pointless, the water slid off the coating without taking any oil with it. I gave up. I had to sacrifice my only towel to scrape the fluid from my flesh, shower with someone else's soap, and air dry. My hair wouldn't clear of the thick, stinking substance for days afterward though I shampooed every morning before crawling into bed.

Every day I looked around at the other red hats working different jobs in the mines and wondered what shit they were getting and how it made them feel. Now and then I'd see one of them get ragged too, but because I was the new guy most of the abuse fell on me. The other guys laughed off the pranks better than I did. I often wondered if they were manning up, fitting in. I looked forward to getting another new guy to take my place at the bottom.

Aaron told me not to take these pranks personally, but I did. He told me the other guys didn't mean any harm, they were having fun, they did this to every new guy, and one day I would do the same to some other red hat. I doubted I would, because the pranks reminded me of the dumbfuck rednecks I went to high school with who used to beat up anyone who wasn't one of them. The pranks reminded me of college, of the hazing rites I witnessed the spoiled fratboys dump on new initiates. I didn't want to be one of them. If that's what it took to get my black hat, to fit in with these men, I wanted no part in it.

I blamed Aaron. He never participated in these pranks, but he let them happen. I was his trainee, and he should have looked out for me, should have warned me these things were coming, but he never did. His silence indicted him.

But Aaron was the nearest I had to a friend during my first four months in the mine, though we weren't what you might call close. Some days we ate lunch together. Other days he ate with the guys and I sat by myself. I carried Kafka's Complete Stories in the bottom of my pail for days like this, but then I had to figure out a system of pointing my cap light at the page, reading the words, and eating my lunch at the same time. The other guys started calling me "professor." And for most of them that was the only word they ever spoke to me. Which was fine; I don't know what we would've talked about.

*

MY FIRST FEW MONTHS IN THE MINES, I CAME HOME EVERY MORNING and Ami was still asleep. Soon after I showered and slid in bed she would wake and go to her job at the hair salon, since she wasn't pregnant enough to stop working yet. By the time she came home, we'd eat dinner in front of the television before I had to leave for the mines. And when I came home the following morning, all the lights would be out and she'd be asleep.

One night, I pulled into the gravel drive that ran up the hill to the back of our house and saw the lights on in every room. I stopped at the back door as always and slid off my boots, leaving them on the stoop. The door was unlocked. When I opened it, a wave of cigarette smoke rolled out. Ami quit smoking when we learned she was pregnant but there was an open pack in a drawer full of rubber bands and forgotten keys, coin wrappers and appliance instructions. A time or two, I thought I'd caught her sneaking one.

When I stepped into the mudroom and shut the door behind me, I knew she'd had more than one. Smoke filled the house and burned my eyes and nose. I walked through the kitchen and into our wood-paneled living room where I found Ami wearing a gray sweatshirt several sizes too large and sitting on the green and orange plaid sofa, her hair pulled up high behind her head, her droopy eyes telling me she hadn't slept and may have cried. On the coffee table in front of her, the ashtray, one of those large purple geode things, was full to bursting. She looked up at me, slid a cigarette out of the open pack beside the ashtray, and lit it.

"Jacob," she said, and the way she said my name told me she had bad news. I took a cigarette from her pack, lit it, and dropped my sore body into the chair to hear what she had to say.

"We lost the baby."

I felt tired. Nothing registered so I didn't say anything.

"It's dead," she said. "I miscarried."

"How do you know?" Probably wasn't the response she wanted, but I was curious. I'd heard of people having miscarriages but didn't know how these things worked.

"How do I know?" she said and started to cry, in an angry way. "Because of the blood, that's how. The fucking blood and the fucking tissue. I've soaked through three pads tonight." Then she started to cry for real, her voice breaking and snot bubbling out of her nose.

I figured I should get up, go to the couch, comfort her. But my body was telling me not to move right then. I didn't know what to say. It's hard to know what to tell someone in a situation like this when you don't feel sad about it too.

I finished my cigarette and stood to crush it out in the geode. I sat beside Ami on the couch and took her by the shoulders and curled her into me. I said all those comforting things I'd practiced saying in other situations with other girls. I stroked her hair. After a few minutes she calmed down and I suggested we go to bed, that we go to the doctor later after we'd slept. She nodded and wiped her nose with the back of her hand. I told her I was going to take a shower.

"Can I pee first?" she said. "Change this pad?"

I told her that was fine and she got up and walked toward the bathroom. Halfway there she fell. Just collapsed. She went down to her knees first and then faceplanted on the carpet. The way she fell looked like a cartoon, so I thought she was joking. She lay there and I didn't know what was happening, so I got worried. I said her name and she said nothing back. I rose and walked over to her and put my hand on her back, said her name again. She started to sit and I helped her, guided her with my hands, not pulling so much as showing her where to go.

"What happened?" she said, rubbing her forehead and looking at me like her eyes couldn't focus.

"You fell down."

"When?"

"Just now."

"I don't remember."

I wanted nothing more at that moment than to sleep and my body felt like it would collapse beside her if I didn't lie down, but she suggested I take her to the hospital. I figured she was right, so I helped her stand and guided her to the car, telling her where to put her feet and encouraging her the whole way.

*

WHEN I TOLD HIM AMI MISCARRIED, I BELIEVE AARON'S SYMPATHY was sincere and I forgave him for not warning me about the pranks. Then he got moved to second shift. I was supposed to be happy for him because he got to work earlier, but I knew I would be lonely.

One morning a guy on day shift was sounding the roof, checking for hollow spots in the rock ceiling by tapping a sounding rod and feeling for vibrations with his fingertips, when a kettle bottom dropped through and killed him. I saw the kettle bottom that did it, this thick slab of petrified shit that must have weighed two hundred pounds or more. My first thought was, better him than me.

Then I learned the guy who died was Joey, one of the rednecks who used to slam me against lockers and vandalize my car and follow me home from school and try to pick fights with me on my girlfriend's lawn. When I found out, I thought it served him right for being a prick.

Since his spot on first shift opened, they moved someone down from second, and they moved Aaron down from third, so I was left without anyone to eat lunch with. Some of the guys feigned interest, asked questions about me. I tried to answer but I could tell they weren't sincere, and the way they laughed made it clear they were mocking me. One day someone took Kafka out of my pail, carried the book to a different room, tossed it on the ground, and pissed on it. I considered quitting on the spot, but Ami's miscarriage had been complicated and ICG paid for our insurance. I felt like the dead baby was haunting me, forcing me to stay in the job it forced me into in the first place.

*

Ami quit the salon after the miscarriage. There were complications, woman stuff. The doctors told her to rest, stay off her feet a while, so we made do on my salary. I felt jealous, wanted to quit my job and stay home all day and sleep and watch TV and burn through packs of cigarettes. I didn't want to be the provider.

The first month, Ami slept most days and nights. When I came home, she'd be in bed, the TV on our dresser tuned to the morning news. I'd shower and lie down beside her and we'd fall asleep together to the voices of the broadcasters. We favored the locals out of Oak Hill and Mount Hope because they didn't flatten their accents. They sounded like family. If she had on the broadcasts out of Charleston or Huntington, I couldn't sleep, their voices too Midwestern and shrill.

The hours between sleep and work, I had to take care of Ami because the complications made her worthless to herself and she looked pathetic. I'd never taken care of anything before. When I was a kid, I begged my dad for a puppy. He told me I could have one if I fed it and walked it and trained it not to crap on the carpet. Of course I didn't, and it ran away. At least that's what he said. When I got older I figured he probably shot it.

That first month after the miscarriage, I did everything for Ami. I learned to cook, though most nights it was something out of a box. I helped her shower, helped her dress. I walked her between the bed and the bathroom and sat her on the toilet. After about a week, I didn't know if she needed help anymore, if her body was still weak and hurting enough, or if she couldn't do these things because her emotions were still screwy. I never asked. She cried often, and I held her and whispered sweet things to her. Then she would fall asleep and I would leave for work.

After that first month, we started having sex again. She told me she felt sore and tender, so I moved slow, gentle. We'd never done it that way. Even after she stopped complaining about pains down there, I kept doing it gentle, and the slowness drove us mad.

One night I kissed her and told her I loved her. It was the first time I meant what I was saying.

Soon, she was up and functioning again, but she stuck to my schedule and we continued to fall asleep to the morning news. We'd wake in the afternoons and spend those hours before work talking. We started eating dinner at the kitchen table instead of the couch. I learned more about her during those few months than I ever had before. I learned about her childhood, about how she was obsessed with horses until she rode one for the first time and it threw her. She said the accident explained her crooked smile. I'd never asked because I always found the imperfection sexy—it was one of the things that first drew me to her. I learned she'd wanted to be a journalist and why she dropped out of high school. She never felt she got it, she said, could never do the work. I felt I knew her now. We'd spent the first few months of our marriage as roommates, friends with benefits. But now she felt like my wife.

She started taking night classes, studied for her GED while I worked. I still hated the job but knew I had something to come home to, and that made the work almost worthwhile.

*

Now THAT AMI WAS MENDING, I SUGGESTED SHE START LOOKING for work once she finished school. If she could find something, I hoped to leave the mines and go into something that paid less but cost me less too. Now it was the two of us again and no baby to care for, I figured we could make ends meet on two small salaries instead of one big one.

Around that time, we got a new guy in the mines. Everyone called him Novak. He was in his thirties, wiry and skittish, the type of guy full of frenetic energy who has to move some part of his body at all times, his hands rubbing, his feet tapping, his eyes running laps in their sockets. When he stood still, he rocked from foot to foot.

Though no one said so outright, I realized it was my responsibility to teach him how to do his job, much like Aaron had done for me. I thought this situation absurd, still wearing my red hat and teaching another red hat. This wasn't protocol—red hats are supposed to be supervised at all times—but the company men could give a damn for protocol.

The first night Novak made all the same mistakes, shining his cap light in everyone's eyes, stumbling in the heavy boots, falling for the pranks. The first time we rode the supplies down to the face, some of the guys convinced him the man ride didn't go back up, and the only way to get to the entry was to ride the belt. So the dumb sonofabitch hopped on the conveyer with the dust and shards of coal. I took the tractor and followed him. The guys told Novak the belt would stop to let him off, but I soon saw him realize the only way down was to jump. He tried to get his footing but kept slipping on the moving belt. In the end, he rolled off and hit the rock floor on his side.

I stopped the man ride beside him. He stood and brushed himself down, his left sleeve torn at the elbow and bloody scraps of skin showing through. He climbed on the tractor beside me.

"Those guys are assholes," I said.

"Heh-heh," he said. "All in good fun."

Novak took everything with that same spirit. I hated him for it. Nothing fazed him, and he whistled while we loaded supplies onto the trailer—the dumb sonofabitch actually whistled while he worked.

Working with Novak was a complete contrast to working with Aaron. Not only were our roles reversed, but Novak never shut his maw. I can say with some certainty that I learned more about Novak in that first night than I did about Aaron in four months.

Like me, Novak had been forced into the job by his family. He'd been a security guard working nights in the psych ward at Appalachian Regional Hospital but when their pay was cut and they went on strike, the owner fired half the staff since they had no union for protection. Novak tried to find work but ended up bagging groceries during the day and mopping floors at the local community college at night. Then his wife birthed a baby more fucked up than church on Saturday, and the child had to have several surgeries so the doctors could repair the spina bifida and stuff her spinal chord inside the vertebrae. She was also born with hydrocephalus, which I'd never heard of but from what I could tell meant she had a large, swollen head. Novak didn't have health insurance after losing his job at the hospital. They lost everything paying for these surgeries to save their tragedy of a baby, so he had to come to the mines to pay off the debt.

After hearing this sob story, I was glad our baby died inside Ami instead of coming out all contorted and deformed.

But Novak, he told me this like he wasn't the least sad about it. He even showed me a photo of his kid—the sonofabitch actually carried the baby's picture with him. The picture showed this floppy looking thing with this giant swollen potato for a head. Of course I lied and said she was cute so Novak would shut up and put the photo back in his breast pocket.

He talked like that the whole shift, telling me how his wife was addicted to a dozen pills, and how his mother had killed his daddy in his sleep and gone off to jail and sent Novak to live with a great-aunt. Real human suffering. Though listening to him, you'd think he was telling you a story of the time he met Elvis's ghost.

Lunchtime came around, and Novak followed me to the dinner hole, blabbering all the way. We sat off to the side and opened our pails and poured coffee into the lids of our thermoses and took out our lunches one item at a time. I told Novak about eating dessert first and he laughed. Then he pointed to the book at the bottom of my pail.

"Never read it," he said.

"You like to read?"

He nodded. "The wife and I read those books on tape. She likes the romance of course, the ones with lots of sex, but I like the courtroom thrillers."

When our lunch break ended, one of the guys from the large group in the middle of the dinner hole turned around, this burly lump with no neck but two extra chins to make up for it.

"Look there boys, at them two red hats," he said, waving toward us. "Couple of baboon's asscracks. Don't they make a pretty couple?" All the men laughed as they gathered their pails.

"Douche bags," I muttered so only Novak could hear.

"Nah," he said. "Just good fun."

I knew what was in store for Novak once we got to the showers, and though I felt responsible, I decided not to warn him. I wanted to see if he took everything as one big joke, if he'd laugh with the bullies. I wanted to see him get angry. I wanted to see him feel the same way

I'd felt every day for the past four months when I took the brunt of their abuse.

Novak was smarter than me. When we went to shower, he put his clean clothes in the basket and raised them to the ceiling. But he left his work clothes piled on the bench in front of his locker. Sure enough, once we'd showered we found the bench empty. We found his boots outside in a ditch and his pants strung over a tree, but we couldn't find his shirt anywhere. I helped him look. Finally the shirt surfaced, stuffed into a toilet.

His smile faded as he pulled the shirt out. When he unsnapped the breast pocket and pulled out the waterlogged picture of his baby, the paper frayed and curling, he looked like he might cry. I mean real, solid tears. While I was glad of the situation, glad to have someone else take their flak, I couldn't help but feel bad for him and regretted letting it happen to a guy who was so damn positive. I found myself saying the same things Aaron said to me about not taking it personally, they do it to all the red hats, that it was all fun and games.

When he turned toward me, the look in his eye told me he wasn't laughing anymore.

"You should have warned me," he said. "You knew this would happen."

His cold tone and calm delivery shocked me out of my brief sympathy. I thought, better him than me.

"Hey pal," I said. "Don't blame me. It was those other guys, the black hats."

"You're just as bad," he said. "You didn't warn me. That makes you guilty, an accomplice. Makes you one of them."

I didn't want him to be right.

*

THAT NIGHT, WHEN I PULLED INTO THE DRIVEWAY, ALL THE LIGHTS in the place were on. Even though Ami waited up for me, she was usually in bed with the lights off and the news on by the time I came home. I didn't think much of it, figured she stayed up studying. I slid my boots from my feet on the back stoop and opened the door into the mudroom. No smoke came out to meet me.

I shut the door behind and called Ami's name. She answered from the living room. When I walked in, she sat on the couch, her fuzzy white bathrobe on and her black hair hanging down the sides of her face. She let her hair grow after the miscarriage and it was longer than I'd ever seen it, falling past her shoulders, almost long enough to cover her nipples when she was topless. The ashtray in front of her was empty, but her cigarettes lay beside it, the lighter balanced atop the softpack. I took one out and lit it before dropping onto the couch beside her.

She gets this look when she has something to tell me, something she's excited about but not sure how I'll respond. She won't look me in the face. Her eyes fall beside my head, looking past me at the wall. She sucks on her bottom lip and says "umm" a lot. That's what she did that night. I asked her what was on her mind. She stalled. Asked how my night was. I told her the same torture as always, told her about Novak and how miserable he made me and what the guys did to him. Then I asked her again what was going on.

She reached into the large pocket of her robe, fingered something, pulled it out, her fist closed around it so I couldn't see. She kept making the face. She opened her hand, palm up, and this plastic stick lay there. I saw the pink cross at one end.

"I'm pregnant," she said.

I said nothing. I smoked my cigarette and looked at her, but her expression had changed. She looked me in the face, expecting something. I dropped my head back on the top of the couch and closed my eyes. She was supposed to be on birth control, told me she was taking it so this wouldn't happen again. I thought about leaving, walking out, quitting her and the mines both, driving away and not coming back to these hills till the end of my days. I thought about suggesting abortion again. I would pay for the procedure before I quit my job, and then I'd make her go on the pill, force it down her throat if I had to.

She said my name, asked me what I thought. I raised my head and looked at her and saw her crooked smile, the lightness of her eyes, and knew she felt happy. It was the happiest I'd seen her since the miscarriage. Hell, it was the happiest I'd ever seen her. I didn't know if I could take that smile from her. I could see my future written across her face. In a couple months I'd have my black hat and even though it would mean Novak was right, my pay and benefits would improve. If I worked hard and proved myself, they'd move me down to second shift in a few years, and a few years after that down to first. And then, many years on, they'd give me one of those brass mining lamps at retirement. I could see that brass lamp shine on her face.

DONATION

WHEN HE HEARD ABOUT THE EXPLOSION THAT KILLED THE TWENTY-nine miners at Upper Big Branch in Montcoal, Ben had been teaching seventh-grade social studies in Baltimore County, Maryland. He wanted to come home as soon as he heard. He knew some of the dead, went to school with some of them and knew others from a childhood in the restaurants and shops of Whitesville. There were few restaurants and shops these days, their storefronts boarded and dusty.

Ben had asked his principal, Ms. Miller, if he could take leave for the rest of the semester to come home and help in any way he could. Ms. Miller refused. The year was almost up, she needed him to stay on. Besides, she said, there was nothing he could do.

By the time school let out, she was right. The funerals had been held, the news crews packed and gone. Whitesville was as deserted as the last time he had been home years before, maybe even more deserted. There was nothing Ben could do. He wanted nothing more than to give the help he knew he could not, but he had missed his chance to be part of it all.

Now two months were gone. He stood inside a gazebo where tributes to the dead hung on or leaned against the walls. Hand-lettered signs, lists of the twenty-nine names, pictures, a drawing of

Christ with his arm around a miner. Ben stared at a black jumpsuit pinned to the far wall. An orange ribbon had been clipped to the chest, and a black miner's cap hung above the coveralls. The person who wore the coveralls would be larger than Ben.

He stepped out of the gazebo and into the vacant lot on the edge of downtown Whitesville. More handmade tributes lay scattered in the grass: Plank crosses, burnt candles, signs, both professional and hand drawn. Ben felt pulled toward a tray filled with chunks of coal. Someone had painted the name of a miner on each chunk in whiteout. More than anything, this choked him.

He turned his back on the memorials and sat on a bench facing the two-lane highway. He watched a man walk the sidewalk across the street, coming from the north end of Route 3 where a chain dollar store stood next to another chain dollar store. The man turned to cross the road. Several dump trucks, loaded high with coal, thundered past. The man seemed to hesitate, to wait for an all clear. He looked weighted down with luggage, a large messenger bag strung across his shoulder and a wheeled suitcase clutched in his hand.

The man stepped into the street, swiveled his head side-to-side, and hurried across. He walked toward Ben and began talking before he reached the bench. "You from around here?" he said

Ben figured him for a motorist with a stalled car and out-of-state tags, someone lost and looking for a way out. "Sure," Ben said. "I grew up here."

Two more coal trucks ground past. Diesel engines revved loud in downshift and tires clomped on the potted tarmac. "I'm a travel punk," the man said.

Ben looked at the man's peach polo and black baseball cap. Ben had not known many punks, but this guy didn't fit his image of ripped jeans, leather jackets, combat boots. "A travel punk?" Ben had to raise his voice above the trucks.

"No," the man shouted. "A traveling monk."

The guy didn't look like a monk either. He wasn't Asian for one thing. For another, he had freckles and the hair on either side of his face was red. Ben had never heard of a redheaded monk. They were supposed to shave their heads, and they didn't have freckles. Ben knew that much.

The man waved at the bench. "Mind if I join you?"

Ben scooted to the side. "Suit yourself."

The monk sat and rested the weight of the messenger bag on the seat between them and wheeled the suitcase around to the side of the bench and left it there to lean. "You ever met a monk before?"

Ben said he had.

"Where?" the guy asked.

"Up in DC."

"At the airport?"

"No." Ben had seen the Krishnas in the airport, seen them with their robes and tambourines and flowers. But he was thinking of a particular monk. "On the National Mall."

That particular monk had looked more like a guru, someone who tripped acid with George Harrison and kept a pet monkey. Long grey hair and beard, sun-dried face. The guru had been naked to the waist and dancing by himself in the middle of the dirt and gravel along the Mall. His bare feet were dark brown and coated in dust. He had no robe, no tambourine. A sheet lay in the grass near him with several knickknacks and books spread out. Ben tried to hurry past him to the Air and Space Museum, but the guru stopped dancing and flagged him down.

The guru talked to Ben for several minutes about the weather. Whenever people talked about the weather, Ben figured they were wasting time, but this guy had a lot to say. He sounded enlightened or stoned. He handed Ben two books, one on the spiritual guidance of another guru and the other a guide to vegan living. He asked for a donation for the books, but when Ben showed his empty wallet, he told him to take them anyway. As Ben left, the guru placed his palms together in front of his chest and said something in some Indian language. Ben hoped it was a blessing instead of a curse.

"He give you a copy of this?"

The monk on the bench pulled a thick hardcover from his messeger bag. The book was orange with a red ribbon sticking out from the bottom of the pages and felt heavy in Ben's hand. The cover was thick and solid, made of something durable, and it showed a blue-faced Indian prince riding the back of a tiger. The tiger looked fierce, its mouth hanging open to show its sharpened teeth, frozen in an eternal snarl. But the prince riding the tiger looked peaceful. His eyes were close set on his blue face and seemed sleepy. He neither smiled nor frowned. The prince looked like he saw the world as it was, saw all the tragedy, but found existence worthwhile. As he stared at the prince's face, Ben felt the first peace since before the explosion.

"This is the *Bhagavad-Gita*," *the monk said. "India's most holy book."*

In college, Ben hooked up with a hippie girl at a friend's party. She had big chocolate eyes and a decent body but was lifeless in bed. Ben thought that was the end, but she materialized on his stoop a few days later, claiming her apartment's pipes had frozen and she needed a place to shower. Before Ben knew what had happened, she began keeping shampoos and clothes and a hair dryer in his apartment. Her road name was Sometimes. Ben never learned her real name. Sometimes was into the whole Eastern thing and talked about the Bhagavad-Gita a lot. Usually after sex. During sex, she didn't talk much.

The monk turned the book to the back cover. His finger pointed to a blurb from Gandhi. "Maybe you've heard of Gandhi," he said. "This was his favorite book." He pointed to two other blurbs. "It was also the favorite book of the American transcendentalists Thoreau and Emerson." He pointed to each of their names beneath the blurbs.

Ben knew all about Thoreau and Emerson. They lived in the woods beside ponds and wrote essays with a lot of unnecessary words. Sometimes loved Thoreau but claimed Emerson was pretentious. She carried a Portable Thoreau in her large patchwork satchel and had the annoying habit of reading passages aloud.

Before Ben broke up with her, Sometimes adopted two stray kittens and named one of them Walden. The other she named Boots.

"We're traveling the country," the monk said, "distributing books to promote peace and harmony." The monk paused, seemed to weigh what he had to say. "We wanted to come here because people are hurting. They could use spiritual guidance."

Ben agreed, people around Whitesville needed spiritual guidance, but he worried that anything involving blue-faced princes riding tigers would be seen as satanic. Ben hadn't considered himself a Christian for many years, even before Sometimes moved into his apartment and refused to leave and brought all her shampoos and mystic weirdness with her. Unlike many people who lived in Whitesville, Ben didn't have spiritual peace to fall back on.

He needed this book. He doubted he would ever read the book, but it was beautiful. The cover was alive with color and motion, unlike the black leather on his Bible. He wanted to see the Bhagavad-Gita sitting on his desk, wanted to hold its cover every night before sleep, flip through its pages, move the ribbon bookmark to different chapters to see how it looked there.

"We're traveling the country giving these to people." The monk removed his baseball cap and ran fingers through his short red hair. He had a bald spot on his crown and freckles on his scalp. "We ask for a small donation." He put the cap back on his head. "So we can print more."

This sounded reasonable. Someone had to pay for printing, and Ben doubted monks could afford those costs. He took the billfold from his back pocket. "I only have a five." He pulled out the bill and showed the monk the empty wallet.

The monk wrenched the book from Ben's hand. "The standard donation for a hardcover is twelve dollars." He crammed the beautiful book into the messenger bag.

Like that, the peace was gone. Ben wanted to see the Bhagavad-Gita again, wanted to hold it in his hands. He held the memory of the book's weight and felt the same way he felt about coming home to Whitesville too late to help.

"But," the monk said, "five dollars is the typical donation for a paperback. Will you take the paperback instead?"

Ben said he would. The monk grabbed the five, slid the bill into the breast pocket of his polo, and pulled a paperback from his satchel. The book was smaller, looked like it would fit in Ben's pocket. The same blurbs from Emerson and Thoreau appeared on the back cover, but the Gandhi quote hadn't made the cut.

The front cover was not orange but blue, the same blue as the face of the Indian prince. Light gray clouds rose behind him all the way to the title. Instead of the tiger, the prince rode on a golden chariot drawn by three white horses, their bent legs kicking swirls of dirt. The prince looked smug, not peaceful like he had on the tiger.

The monk rose from the bench, hoisted the messenger bag onto his shoulder, and grabbed the wheeled suitcase. He began to walk away but turned back. "Have a blessed day."

Ben felt disappointed with the book in his hand, like it was no book at all, and the monk's farewell left him run through. Ben wished the monk would at least say something in a foreign language, something peaceful.

The monk dragged his luggage down the sidewalk, headed south on Route 3 toward Pettus, Naoma, Montcoal, Dry Creek. Ben wondered if the monk would travel that far and whether anyone would buy that beautiful book. Ben hadn't driven down the Coal River Valley since coming home. Maybe he'd follow the monk's trail. Maybe there he would find someone who still needed whatever Ben could give.

HELL AND HIGH WATER

GILLIAN AND HER PARENTS DO NOT LEARN WHAT HAPPENED TO GUS until he comes home to Black Bear Creek in July and brings Dixie with him. They know he stopped attending class soon after the spring semester began and then left Morgantown all together, but they didn't hear from him for months. They called the school every few weeks. The administration could tell them he quit the team, dropped his classes, moved out of the dorm, but nothing more. Where he went and what he did for those months after, Gillian never learns. Somewhere along the way he found Dixie, and when he comes home he claims to have taken her for wife.

The family sits in the small living room of their frame house and Gillian stares at the girl returned with her brother. Dixie is tall, she sits almost as tall as Gus, and her sandy-blonde hair hangs straight to the middle of her back. Gillian doubts she weighs 100 pounds. Her collarbone shows thin and firm beneath the flimsy-strapped tanktop she wears, and the hollow of her pelvis sinks beneath her tight jeans. Her concave cheeks remind Gillian of a young Joni Mitchell.

Dad asks to see the marriage certificate.

"They never give us one," Gus says.

"Until you show me a license," Dad says, "you don't sleep together under my roof."

Gus protests while Dixie sits by, looking at her hands, until Mom pulls a camping mat from the closet, motions for the girls to follow her upstairs, and unrolls it on Gillian's bedroom floor.

"I'll find bedding," Mom says and leaves them in the small room. Gillian sits on the edge of her bed and listens to Gus and Dad argue downstairs. Dixie stands leaned against the wall between the door and desk, and she fidgets with the dirt under her nails.

"How old are you?" Gillian asks.

"Eighteen," Dixie responds without looking from her fingers. "How old are you?"

"Fourteen," Gillian says. "How old are you really?"

Dixie looks up. "I'll be sixteen in October."

Gillian can hear the raised voices of the men downstairs, until there's a pause, a still, broken when the front door slams. On cue, she hears Mom's soft footfall up the stairs, and as she turns the corner into Gillian's room her arms are wrapped around a pile of blankets, pillows, and sheets. She drops the burden on the camping mat, turns to Dixie, and smiles the forced smile Gillian has seen all her life whenever Mom acts courteous or professional.

"You're welcome to stay as long as you like," Mom says. "Until we get this straightened out."

Dixie thanks her. Mom tells them goodnight and goes downstairs. Gillian hears the television, the news out of Oak Hill that Dad watches every night. Dixie arranges the sheets and blankets on the camping mat and stuffs the pillows into their cases.

"Do you have a toothbrush?" Gillian asks.

Dixie shakes her head, no.

"You can use my old one."

*

WHEN GILLIAN WAKES THE NEXT MORNING, SHE LOOKS OVER THE edge of her mattress to see Dixie on the floor, her eyes open, studying the ceiling. "Morning," Gillian says.

"You snore."

"No I don't," she says. "Do I?"

"You talk, too."

"What did I say?"

"Mumbles. But it sounded important, like you were desperate."

Gillian sits up, pulls the thin quilt and sheet down, stretches her arms above her head, and makes a sound like a cat. She hopes this makes her seem cute—a move she's practiced, but never used. Dixie lies still on the camping mat.

"No one's ever told me that," Gillian says.

"You never snuck a boyfriend up here for the night?"

Gillian feels flushed. "No."

"No? You never have girlfriends sleep over?"

"Not since I was a kid."

"You got to make friends."

Gillian wonders how many friends Dixie has, how many boyfriends she's snuck into her room in the middle of the night. She wonders where these friends and boyfriends are now, and why she left at sixteen to follow Gus to this holler if she was so popular back home, wherever home is. Gillian wants to ask where she's from, where her people are, but something about Dixie—her voice, her body language, her forced smile—says she does not like questions and likes answers even less.

They eat a light breakfast in the empty kitchen, the sounds of *The Young and the Restless* coming through the wall. Dad's at work, hauling coal for Massey in the heavy truck. The door to Gus's room, off the kitchen, stands open, the bed still made. Gillian wonders where he passed the night. She studies Dixie's face, curious to know how she feels now that Gus left her there alone. Dixie's face shows nothing.

After they eat, she and Dixie walk out of the holler, across the wooden bridge that spans the thin creek, down the gravel road that intersects Route 3. They turn up the two-lane highway running toward Beckley. Traffic rolls by light but loud, mainly large trucks hauling coal up the mountain.

They approach Milam's service station. The white clapboard building stands with a shallow parking lot and two fuel pumps in front of it. They mount the few stairs leading up to the front porch of the store, pass the empty chairs where the old men often sit and smoke and chew the fat over foam cups of Milam's weak coffee.

Inside, past the register with racks of cigarettes and chewing tobacco behind and past the local post office window and rows of mailboxes with old combination turn locks, a short lunch counter spans the rest of the narrow store. Mrs. Milam and Mrs. Jarrell sit at two of the five stools, drinking coffee and eating egg sandwiches. The women are sisters and they wear the uniform of the Holiness church, the long denim skirts trailing their shins, canvas shoes and white ankle socks showing at the bottom, plain T-shirts. Both wear their thin gray hair tied into buns at the base of their skulls. Gillian knows their hair would reach below their waists if not for the buns.

She went to a Holiness church once, as a child, with a friend. She could barely keep from laughing at the way the women wept and ran the aisles screaming, the way the men spoke the tongues. For weeks after, she imitated the preacher, how he hiccupped the sermon's every word, how he accentuated every syllable. "Jee-Suss-Ah," she repeated until Mom banned Holiness from the house.

They take seats at the end of the counter, one stool between them and the two women. "How are you, Mrs. Milam, Mrs. Jarrell?" Gillian asks. They nod. Gillian orders a Diet Coke and Dixie a coffee, black.

Mrs. Milam turns and looks Dixie once over. "You must be the girl shacked up with the Petty boy. What's your name, honey?"

Gillian knows gossip travels fast in Black Bear Creek, but this speed shocks her. When Dixie replies, Mrs. Jarrell mumbles into her cup, "What sort of people name a child Dixie?"

Before she can defend herself, Mrs. Milam asks "Dixie what?"

"Toler."

"Toler? Must be from Wyoming County."

"My dad's people are from Pineville, I think."

Mrs. Milam closes her eyes and bows her head in affirmation, as though she knew this already, could smell it on the girl. Gillian thinks about the stories she'll tell Dixie when they walk home. How it's common knowledge that on the eve of their wedding, Mrs. Jarrell's husband, a fireboss for Massey, slept with her sister, and how Mrs. Jarrell seems to be the only person in town who does not know, or at least doesn't let on she knows. Or how Mrs. Milam's husband, the storeowner, got caught in an awkward situation with the babysitter when the girl's boyfriend walked in on them. How the Milams fired the girl since this proved she snuck her boyfriend over when they entrusted her with their children. Sets a bad moral example, Mrs. Milam explained to Mom.

They finish their drinks and pay. Gillian drops an extra dollar on the counter for tip. She tells the two women to have a good day.

"Tell your Mom hello," Mrs. Milam says. "Tell her the church is holding a rummage sale next Sunday."

Gillian thanks Mrs. Milam and assures her she will pass on the news. As she says these goodbyes, she sees, in her periphery, Dixie swipe the tip off the counter and pocket the bill in her tight jeans.

*

THAT AFTERNOON, GUS HAS NOT RETURNED, BUT HE SHOWS UP IN time for dinner, shortly after Dad comes home from work. Mom brings the dishes piled with chicken-fried steak and boiled potatoes and corn to the table where the rest of the family and Dixie sit. Each dish passes from hand to hand, and each person scoops out a portion before passing it along.

Dad and Gus do the talking, ignore the tense topics. They talk sports, weather, movies. The conversation turns to Gus's attempt to make the WVU roster.

"Those boys are like you wouldn't believe," Gus says. "I couldn't hang with them."

Gillian grew up watching Gus's games every summer. He was taller and stronger than most boys his age, a natural lefty with a quick fastball, though his curve lacked break and he tipped the changeup. Once in Babe Ruth league he tagged a kid on the Hinton team with a pitch that got away from him. It rose hard and fast and caught the kid on his left temple before he could duck, rendering him blind. Gillian expected this to eat away at Gus, but he dismissed it as a risk of the game. If he internalized the guilt, he never showed it to his little sister.

"Every pitch I threw, they knocked out of the park," Gus says between mouthfuls of food. "Coach wanted to try me at left field, but I told him it's the mound or nothing."

Gillian finds this foolish since the family counted on Gus earning a spot on the roster and a partial scholarship if not more, but Dad seems proud, grinning at Gus as they cut their meat and stuff it in mashed potatoes before cramming it into their jaws.

After they exhaust sports, Dad brings up employment. "If you're going to live here," he says, "you need a job. Tomorrow you'll go with me, see if they've got a spot for you. They won't let you drive, not at first, but maybe they'll let you load."

Dixie looks at Dad and then at Gus. "I don't think you should work for the mines," she says. Gillian turns from Dixie to her parents in wonder. Neither she nor Gus has ever talked back to Dad, because they know his temper. Mom drops her eyes and pushes the flat of her fork into the mashed potatoes.

Dad sets his silverware down on the plate. "Excuse me?" It's the first he's addressed her since they were introduced the night before.

"Gus has so much talent," Dixie says. "He's so smart. I don't want to see him waste it working for a company like Massey. They tear down the mountains and cause all the problems in this state."

"Massey provides for this state," Dad says. "If it weren't for Massey, you wouldn't have this food. Would you have this family starve?"

"I was thinking," Gus says, "I'd get up in the morning and go see Mr. Milam about my old job."

Dad finishes his long, hard look at Dixie before turning to Gus. "That'll do," he says. "For the time being."

"I saw the prettiest robin today," Mom says. "She came right up to the feeder in front of the window."

*

THE NIGHTS THAT FOLLOW, GILLIAN WAKES TO THE SOUND OF HER door opening. The first time, she assumes Dixie needs the bathroom, but she hears soft steps down the stairs and Gus's door open and shut below. The first few nights, she accepts these meetings as natural. When she wakes in the morning, Dixie's asleep on the mat on the floor.

But several nights in, she lies unable to sleep after her door opens. She stares at the darkness and wonders what it must be like when they hold one another, when they move into and out of one another. What faces Gus must make. What pleas Dixie must utter. Her twin bed has never seemed so vast and she has never felt so lonely. She begins to cry though she hates herself for crying.

*

THE MORNING GUS STARTS AT MILAM'S, SHE AND DIXIE WAKE EARLY and walk to the store for breakfast. Though only a few hours old, the day is warm and humid, and the wind rolling down Coal River Mountain blows sticky against them. They cross Milam's parking lot and into the store, whose air conditioner hasn't worked for three summers. The open door and oscillating fans bring in more heat.

Gus stands behind the counter wearing his faded WVU cap, its bill frayed along the edge, and a crisp white apron he managed to stain in his first hour on the job. He stands with his arms at shoulder width, his palms on the counter's edge, and he talks to Mrs. Milam and Mrs. Jarrell, who occupy their usual stools. When he looks up at them, he smiles in a way Gillian's never seen, more genuine than the catalogue of smiles she compiles in memory.

Dixie leaves her side and runs around the counter, wraps her arms around Gus's neck, and presses her mouth to his. When Gus encircles her back with his arms, she raises her legs from the floor so he has to hold her suspended. Gillian blushes in embarrassment for them. But the couple don't seem to mind. Not until Mr. Milam harrumphs from the register do they stop.

Gus serves them eggs and bacon and thick coffee in heavy chipped chinaware. Gillian empties two packets of sweetener and a plastic tub of creamer into her mug and stirs until the liquid cools, but Dixie drinks the stuff black and steaming. She drains her second mug before Gillian finishes her first.

After their breakfast, Dixie leans across the counter and pulls Gus to her for another kiss, and they start their walk. The day before, Dixie made her take an oath that they will exercise every morning, to lose weight. Gillian assumes this is for her sake, since Dixie can hardly stand to get skinnier. Gillian's never considered herself fat, but the way Dixie looked at her when she suggested they exercise makes her reconsider.

The heat rises steaming from the blacktop highway and the creek that ambles alongside, road and river curving to accommodate the mountains rolling down in every direction. The trees that clothe the slopes ripple with the breeze, exposing the dark undersides of their green leaves like the rolling shadow of some passing airship. More than once, she catches Dixie scanning the sky for the shadow's source. Thirty minutes in, Gillian's calves burn, her side stitches, and she laments the sludgy coffee and greasy food sloshing in her guts. They walk the winding road three miles to Marsh Fork Elementary in Sundial. Gillian never expected the sight of the school where she spent six years to bring such relief.

They sit on swings in the shadow of the coal silo that looms behind the school. Coal dust powders the playground like black snow. When Gillian stretches her feet before her, she sees the soot has stained the white canvas of her tennis shoes. She looks at Dixie's feet in their sandals, and her soles and insteps are covered the same.

"Where does it come from?" Dixie asks when Gillian calls the dust to her attention.

"The silo," she says and points behind them. "They load trains there."

"I can't believe they put it so close to the school."

Dixie stands and walks toward the silo, and Gillian follows. As they approach, blasts echo down from the short rise two hundred yards beyond. They both turn their heads toward the sound. Dixie says nothing for several minutes, then bows and shakes her head. "I can't believe people live where they mine. Why don't you move?"

Gillian considers how to respond. She's never questioned her home, and Dixie's tone offends her. "We don't live where they mine," she says. "They mine where we live."

*

Every night the following week, Dixie sleeps with Gillian, blaming a fight she had with Gus. Gillian asks its cause, but Dixie tells her men can be stupid and will say no more. They try their best not to touch, but the twin bed makes this difficult. They try sleeping head to foot, but Gillian wakes throughout the night with Dixie's dirty toes in her hair. The next night they give up and curl together, taking turns being the bigger spoon, arms around the other's waist, legs bent inside the bend of the other's legs. Gillian has never slept as soundly as she does when she presses her face to the hollow between Dixie's shoulders.

They talk late into the night. They forgo their morning walks and instead sleep in, lounge around the house, eat junk food. They promise atonement with longer walks the next day and then the next.

Dixie curled around her, Gillian confesses she always wanted a sister.

"I have four," Dixie says. "Sisters are overrated."

*

They forget their oath of exercise. They spend the hot afternoons at the counter in Milam's or sunning in the field around the house or seeking the shade of the woods when they can take no more. They dip their feet in the creek, recline on their elbows planted in the shore.

"When I was a kid," Gillian begins.

"You're still a kid."

"Shut up." Gillian pushes her sideways, one-handed. "When we were kids, Gus and I used to hunt crawdads in this crick. Gus had to lift the rocks when they swam under—I was scared they'd bite."

They debate whether it's crawfish, crayfish, or crawdad, having heard and used all three. The water runs cool across Gillian's bare feet, and the shade of the copse keeps the sunlight from her skin.

Gillian feels something brush her toe, jerks her foot from the water. Dixie laughs.

"Sorry," she says. "Just me."

Gillian feels Dixie's foot against hers in the water. It comforts her now that she knows it is no crustacean. It excites her.

"I bet Gus was a good brother," Dixie says. "He'll make a good daddy someday."

Gillian scratches her nose. "He was okay, I guess. He never beat me up."

"Me neither." The way Dixie says it makes Gillian wonder if this is a first, if this qualifies as love.

"What do you see in my brother? Why did you follow him to this place?"

At first, Dixie stays quiet. Gillian worries she offended her.

"I would follow him anywhere," Dixie says.

"Hell or high water?"

Dixie nods. "Hell and high water."

*

A FEW NIGHTS LATER, SHE LISTENS TO DIXIE DESCEND THE STAIRS and then climb them again. When Dixie opens her bedroom door, Gillian sits bolt upright, can make out only the dark form of the other girl. Dixie sits on the edge of her bed by Gillian's knees.

"He's gone," she says.

Gillian starts to ask where he went but realizes how stupid she would sound. She reaches out, touches Dixie's neck, shoulder, runs her fingers through the tips of her hair. "He'll be back," she says. She can make out the dullest features of Dixie's face. The curve of her nose and forehead, the hollows of her cheeks and eye sockets.

"I don't know," Dixie whispers. "He's—gone."

Gillian's eyes adjust and she can see the girl's features in the blue light of darkness. She knows this image, the shadows falling across Dixie's face, the distant, empty expression of fear and sorrow.

*

WHEN SHE WAKES, SHE FINDS DIXIE SITTING ON THE CAMPING MAT, her arms wrapped around her knees. Whether she woke early or never slept, Gillian doesn't know. She doubts she'd get an answer if she asked.

Dixie says next to nothing as they dress and brush their teeth. Gillian asks if she wants to go to Milam's, and Dixie only nods. When they walk through the front door, the three heads at the lunch counter turn toward them.

"There she is now," Mrs. Milam says.

"Speak of the devil," Mrs. Jarrell mumbles. "Or devils."

Behind the counter, where Gus normally smiles at them as they sit and eat the food he cooks, Mr. Milam stands wearing the stained white smock. Gillian thinks he looks tired and angrier than she can remember.

"Gillian," he says. "You know where that brother of yours is?"

"No sir," she says. "Haven't seen him since yesterday."

Gillian sits on her normal stool but Dixie doesn't sit beside her. She stands behind, to the side. The Milams look from one girl to the other.

"What about you, honey?" Mrs. Milam says. "You know where Gus run off to?"

Gillian turns and waits for her answer. Dixie stands and stares at Mrs. Milam with a look like she doubts the question is meant for her or doesn't know the language to respond.

Mrs. Jarrell makes a sound like psht, waves her hand at them, and turns back to her coffee. "Maybe he run off with another girl," she says. "One with a Christian name."

Gillian rises, takes Dixie by the hand, and walks toward the door. Her arm grows taut. She turns and sees Dixie standing there, staring at the women before her. Gillian pulls on her gently.

"Has anyone ever told you you're ugly?" Dixie asks Mrs. Jarrell. "You're the ugliest woman I ever seen."

Gillian pulls her arm harder, drags her to the door. Not letting her hand go, Gillian leads her home.

*

HER ARMS AROUND DIXIE'S WAIST, HER LEGS FOLLOWING THE BEND of Dixie's legs, Gillian feels the heat from their bodies blend under the thin covers. The night is sticky, but the skin of Dixie's arms is cool. Gillian cannot sleep. From the sound of her breath, neither can Dixie. Gillian looks around the room, the parts of it she can see around the body beside her, and tries to make out each object in the dark.

Dixie rolls over, her expression solemn and reverent, her eyes open. They stare at one another for some time, and neither speaks. The heat of Dixie's breath makes Gillian feel she can't breathe, and Dixie's deep stare makes her feel uncertain.

Dixie sighs and her eyes close and she presses her cold lips softly against Gillian's for a tick of the moment-hand before rolling away to her side of the bed. Gillian takes breath and holds it until she must let it out. She doesn't know what to do or what the kiss means. Her first kiss and it disappoints her. She expected more. She expected some understanding, some meaning, some clear definition of love or lust. But she doubts Dixie feels either.

She drifts into light, troubled sleep wondering about the kiss. She wakes when she feels the weight on the bed shift and Dixie's side of the mattress rise. She leaves her eyes closed and listens to the sounds of her door opening, footfalls down the stairs, and the front door open and shut.

She counts to one hundred before opening her eyes, tells herself she'll hear the front door open again before she finishes counting. She is disappointed when she counts the final number in her head and looks out into darkness. As each object fades into view, she tells herself Dixie will come back before she can see the next one. She is disappointed dozens of times over.

The last item her eyes focus on is a slip of paper on her nightstand. She sits up, reaches for it, feels the paper cool and wrinkled like an old dollar bill. She counts again before unfolding it, then waits for her eyes to detect the letters on the page, turning it this way and that in front of the window. Words fade in one after the other.

Sorry, kid. I have to find him. You'll know this one day.

Gillian folds the page, returns the note to its place on the nightstand. She sits in her bed the rest of the night, wondering what to name the emotions she feels. She cries some, but not as much as she would expect. She feels too hollow to cry.

When dawn draws through her bedroom window, she rises, pulls the sheet and blankets across the bed and tucks their edges under the mattress. She lifts the note, crumbles it, drops it into the wastebasket. She strips the bedding from the camping mat, pulls the pillow from its case, and carries the bundle downstairs to the laundry.

When she returns to her room, she rolls up the mat and fastens the thin blue cam straps around it. She starts to take the mat downstairs and put it back in the hall closet but decides to leave it propped there in the corner of her bedroom, in easy reach if Dixie ever comes home or if Gillian ever decides to take off in the night after a love she cannot imagine.

TRIBUTE

THE FRONT LABEL ON THE PLASTIC VODKA BOTTLE HAS A RUSSIAN name, but the back label says it was brewed in Baltimore. I went to Baltimore once when I was a teenager and don't much care to drink anything made from Baltimore water. But the vodka was cheap and will do its job, so I bought a handle on my way to the mine.

Before Riley got sick, me and Sheila each had day jobs, she a secretary and me a mine guard for Massey. I kept the hippie protestors out, and the reporters. Sheila quit her job spring before last and they started their garden. To provide for my family and the hospital bills, I asked the boss for a transfer to nights because the shift pays better. They didn't have any night work except for the abandoned mines waiting to be blasted shut. So now I sit in my car at the entrance to a different abandoned shaft every few months to make sure the teenagers stay out. Kids will find any place to get stoned and screw.

I used to leave before dark and come home before daybreak, take a nap, wake and drink coffee while I watched Sheila and Riley dig around in the backyard, waiting for anything to grow. Then I'd shower and take another nap, eat dinner, and back to my car parked at the mouth of the abandoned mine.

Not much has changed since Riley left us. Sheila is the only one who digs around in what used to be the garden, and now I keep a bottle under the seat. At first it was Wild Turkey, cheap whiskey to keep off the winter cold, I told myself. But one night I guess I dozed off. I was half asleep and full drunk when someone knocked on the driver side window. I started up fast and thought I was a dead man for a second, thought for sure it was someone wanting to rob and shoot me for meth money.

"The hell, Roscoe? You sleeping?"

It was my boss, this wiry s.o.b. calls himself Buddy, though I don't know anyone who's his pal. Like all bosses, he's this wimpy little shit with a mustache and a mouth bigger than his body, and he's used to getting what he wants since he has the money to afford it. I knew I was up the creek, so I took a pull from the Turkey before I screwed the cap on and stowed the bottle under my seat.

"Is that booze? Are you drinking?" Buddy said. "What in the name of God Almighty got into you?"

I opened up the door and almost hit him with it. He took a step back, still cussing me. I stood out of the car and raised to my full height. If he wanted a go, he was going to get one.

"Are you drunk?"

I didn't bother to lie. I didn't see the point, and didn't much care one way or the other. He yelled at me for a while, called me all sort of names, until I reminded him he was cussing a drunk with nothing to lose, and he shut up for a minute. Then he cussed me some more, told me to go home, sober up, told me to come to his office in the morning and we'd talk about my future with Massey Energy. But the little bastard didn't have the guts to fire me, especially not when he was faced with the thought of having to find some other idiot willing to sit in a parked car outside a dugout mine and wait for something to happen.

Since then I've switched. They say vodka is harder to smell.

*

I STAND THERE IN MY UNDERPANTS LOOKING OUT THE BACK WINDOW and watch my wife dig this hole. She starts simple enough, shovel in hand, breaking earth and tossing it to the side. By the time I brew my coffee, she's dug a good size trench and stands in it to her shins. Then she starts to widen and stretch the hole about as long as a child laid out. Then she digs down, deeper, tosses clay with soil, like the dig and pull and toss is all she knows.

April and the wind's still cool, but I can see she sweats in a slant of evening sun. What makes her labor? What devil rides her?

I never seen Sheila dig like this. She's dug in the yard for the better part of the year, planted all sort of odds and ends, but she always used a garden trowel. This morning she handles my shovel, the one I used to pry out all the rocks and roots so she and Riley could start their garden two springs past. I wonder what needs a hole so deep.

I sip at my coffee. I consider going out to stop her, but she seems to have purpose, so I let her alone. She's up to her knees and still digging, the pile of dirt and clay growing. I look at her, the muck and sweat covering her, the red of her face and neck, her eyes focused on the shovel's thrust and pull. She mumbles to herself, which makes me sad and helpless. Not because of Riley, I've been sad about that for months, but because Sheila's all but gone too and there's not a thing I can do to save her when she's so bent on losing herself.

I turn from the window and make cereal and open the Sunday paper. Today's Tuesday, but we get only the Sunday paper out of Beckley, The Register-Herald. Sunday papers carry more good news and human-interest stories. I read them, but I don't pay attention to what I read. Used to be, I'd play this game where I'd read aloud the obituaries and Sheila and I would laugh at all the folk who'd been called to heaven or went to meet their maker or became angels. No one ever dies in the obituary pages. But I haven't been able to laugh at the obituary game these days, and I know Sheila would never think to speak of me again if I was to read her someone else's obit.

She wouldn't yell at me, not anymore. Used to be, we needed very little cause to fight. One wrong word or look or some imagined slight and out would come all the hateful, nasty stuff we'd never imagine saying to another living soul, all those names we reserved for each other. But all the fight seems to have drained out of Sheila since Riley passed. Mad as she gets at me, she won't say a word.

I go back to the window when I've ate. She stands out of the hole, the dirt and clay stacked to her waist. She stabs the shovel blade in the pile of dirt, wipes her hands on her cutoff jeans, and wanders around the side of the house. A minute later she comes round the corner, bent near double, pushing Riley's Big Wheel in front of her.

She pushes it to the edge and stops and looks down to the hole. She stands there a minute, then tosses the Big Wheel over the edge. Without any sort of fanfare, the front wheel topples down into the hole. The plastic trike pauses with its rear end tipped up in the air before it falls ass over elbows and disappears.

From when he was a baby, Riley'd loved anything with wheels. I wanted to get him the Big Wheel because it'd been my favorite when I was a kid. I rode that thing up and down the gravel road leading to my people's property on Coal River Mountain, on the ridge above the plot of land Sheila and I bought when we married. I would ride down the slopes toward Black Bear Creek, then push the plastic tricycle back up, and go down again. One day I tried to cross the shallows and cracked the front wheel on a rock. Daddy tanned my hide and refused to buy me another one, and my sisters wouldn't let me ride theirs.

"Not in hell, Roscoe," they said. "We seen what you done to yours." My sisters were always that way.

I looked in several stores for Riley's Big Wheel, but I guess they stopped making them. We found one at a yard sale. The tassels were torn off the handlebars, and I had to glue the seat down in back, but it rolled fine and the pedals turned easy even if the axle was rusted. Riley spent so many hours driving circles around the house, he wore the grass down to a track of dirt.

Sheila grabs up the shovel and starts filling the hole. I set my mug down on the counter. I'm in for a long night.

*

RILEY LOVED ALL MY FAVORITE TOYS FROM WHEN I WAS A KID. IN yard sales we found him several dozen G.I. Joes and a few sandwich bags of plastic guns and helmets and backpacks. I'd watch him build small hills in the dirt of the backyard and stage battles that lasted the day. The G.I. Joe cartoon had gone off the air by then and most of the insignia had worn off, so he didn't know who were good guys and who were bad, except Cobra Commander, who no one would mistake for a hero. So he made it up as he went, gave them names and decided if they were bad or good by the look of their faces. As the battles drew on, he'd bury the dead in the patch of dirt he used for a boneyard and stick their guns out of the ground, their helmets dangling on top for tombstones.

When Riley watched TV he'd take one of his G.I. Joes and twist the legs and hips in circles while holding the torso in place. Once he'd wound them tight, he'd let go the legs and watch them spin. Breakdancing, he called it. After a few spins, the rubber bands inside would snap and the toy would break apart. He'd gather the pieces and ask me to make them whole. Surgery, he called it. I'd remove the screw in the middle of the back to open the torso, put a new rubber band through it, and attach the hook from the legs to the other end of the band. Regular flat rubber bands never worked as well as the black round ones the factory used, but it was enough to keep him happy.

*

I COME OUT OF THE SHOWER AND WRAP A TOWEL ROUND MY WAIST. The mirror's slick with fog. I run my hand across it leave a streak of glass, and think about shaving. The glass fogs over again, and my face disappears. I think against shaving and walk into the hall still wet.

Sheila's in the kitchen now, standing at the window staring at the hole she dug and filled. Her shirt's soaked through with sweat, and she's covered in dirt and clay. She's worked the muck into her hair. Even with her that grimy and me clean and showered, I think about coming up behind her, putting my arms around her like I would've done when we were younger, when we first married. Before we had Riley. But I know she wouldn't like it, would pull away like she's done since he's been gone. She'd complain that I'd get her wet. Or more likely, she'd say nothing and walk off to the bathroom.

I move past her to the fridge and get out what I need to make my lunch. Dinner, I guess, but when you work nights none of your meals have the right names. I put my hand on the knob of a cupboard to take down the bread, but I remember that isn't where Sheila keeps it anymore. Now she keeps it in the drawer beneath the silverware drawer.

After the funeral they took the little coffin and burned him in it and gave us this urn with his ashes and the casket's ashes mixed together. We couldn't agree where to scatter them—Sheila pushed for the garden, I pushed for the creek where I took him fishing, and neither of us gave—so the urn sits in that empty cupboard waiting for us to decide. I think we put the urn there so we wouldn't have to look at what was left of him. Guess I should say I was the one who put him there.

I make my sandwich and watch her without letting her know I'm watching. We don't say anything. I put the sandwich in my metal tin and start a pot of coffee for my thermos. She sets her empty glass in the sink and starts past me. I reach my arm across her belly and put my hand to her hip and try to make her pause. I want her to stand still and love me again, even for a second.

She doesn't look at me. Since she won't agree to loving, I try the other route. I ask her what the hell she was doing out there. "I saw you," I say, my hand still on her hip. "I watched you bury his Big Wheel."

I want to hurt her. Not physically—I never touched her in a hurtful way and I'm not about to start now. But I want to make her angry enough to yell at me, to call me names again, all those horrible names she used to call me. Cocksucker, bastard. Trash. Anything. I want to hurt her bad enough to make her feel something, so she'll remember how she used to feel about me before we lost him. But I don't know anything I can say that will hurt her without hurting me worse, so I don't say a further word.

She brushes my hand away and goes down the hall to the bathroom. I stand just as I am. The shower turns on, and the water heater starts to whine. If I followed her, if I busted into the bathroom,

I know she wouldn't be able to ignore me. She'd have to yell at me or let me climb into the shower with her or both. Either way I'd get what I want.

The doorknob won't turn. She locked it behind her. I'm madder than I can remember being in months so I hit the wall hard with the flat of my hand right next to the doorjamb, a loud thump that I feel all the way up to my elbow. I'm madder still, but she doesn't stir inside the bathroom. The only sound is water hitting the tub.

*

SHEILA HAD THE IDEA TO START THE GARDEN WHEN RILEY GOT SICK. I dug out the rocks and roots and we went to a nursery for seed. The two of them would spend hours planting. Sheila would dig a little hole with the trowel and Riley would drop one seed in each hole. He was a careful kid. He read up on vegetables and measured to make sure each hole was far enough from the next. He regulated water and fertilizer and asked me to lay strips of copper to keep slugs out.

That first year, the garden yielded a small crop of tomatoes and string beans and cabbage. The corn never made it, but Sheila promised to keep trying. Riley loved corn on the cob, even when his mother had to cut the kernels off when he lost his baby teeth.

One day after the arrangements were over, I woke and Sheila was in the yard in her bathrobe, digging in the ground, which frost had covered that morning. I went out to see what she thought she was doing, to yell at her that nothing would grow if she planted that early. "The moon's still new," I said. "And the dogwoods ain't even bloomed."

She looked at me like I was the crazy one.

"What the hell you planting?"

She held out her hand. On her palm were several popcorn kernels and a few roasted coffee beans. I didn't know anything I could say to that, so I stood and watched as she finished and then we went inside together.

For weeks after the funeral, I watched Sheila sneak stranger things into the garden—stray buttons, shiny pebbles and shells from a filled bottle in the bathroom, loose change. It was the damnedest thing I ever saw, but I kept quiet, let her grieve in her own way.

One day in late March, I woke up and found Sheila digging in the backyard again. She always dug in the morning while I slept. I made a cup of coffee and went to the window to watch her, wondering what she was planting this time. Beside her, I saw the plastic toolbox Riley kept his G.I. Joes in. Sheila reached her hand into the toolbox, dropped something in a hole, and covered it up before digging the next. I set my mug by the sink and went out the sliding door.

She knelt in the patch of garden Riley had sectioned off for beans. Smears of dirt streaked her arms and she'd smudged the back of her neck under her brown hair pulled into a ponytail. When I got close to her, she dropped Cobra Commander into a hole, filled it in, and started digging another six inches away.

"What in hell?" I said. "Those are Riley's." She hadn't let me touch his room, wouldn't listen about boxing up his clothes or toys.

She looked at me. I saw she had a thumbprint of dirt between her eyes, and streaks of tears stained her cheeks. She seemed not to understand my question, so I repeated it. She dropped her eyes from me, looking confused and put-upon, and picked up another of the plastic soldiers.

"I know," she said. She didn't say anything else, just went back to planting.

That night, as I sat in my car in front of the mine and pulled from the bottle of Wild Turkey, I knew what I had to do. When I got home before dawn, I dug all his G.I. Joes from the garden. The next night, I cleared a place there in that abandoned mine where I could visit Riley's things when I needed him near.

*

THE NIGHTS AREN'T AS BAD AS SOME MIGHT THINK. I'VE PASSED THE year reading books by the glow of the dome light. Mostly nonfiction, especially the science type. I always liked science, did well in it at school. I could've gone to college, probably studied science and made something of myself, but I met Sheila and she was all I ever wanted. Then we had Riley, and then we didn't. Besides, Daddy couldn't afford college, and I never worked hard enough to get a scholarship.

Sometimes I don't understand what I read. Tried that Hawking guy, but none of it was something I could touch. Right now I'm reading this book called The World Without Us, about what the Earth will be like once we're all dead and gone. Skyscrapers falling and wild predators eating all our pets, now that I can understand. All we'll leave behind are the billion tons of plastic we've made.

Reading is fine unless the bosses come round to check on things. Don't know what I'm supposed to do to keep from sleep, but reading ain't an option. Neither is drinking. Tonight ain't so cool, so I'm trying my hand at chasing the vodka with swigs of Mountain Dew, and old Vlad sure treats me right.

I turn the pages and take swigs from the handle. I read but I don't understand what I read, too distracted and jumpy. The mountain's foggy and there's a floodlight on some street behind the woods. The light comes all silver and smoky through the trees and reminds me of stories my grandma used to tell us while we canned vegetables. I don't know that I believe in haints, but when the fog's thick like this I can't help but believe. Then I think about Riley and wish I didn't.

*

WHEN IT'S BEEN LONG ENOUGH THAT SHEILA SHOULD BE GOOD AND asleep, I leave the mine and head back to our place. I pull slow up the gravel drive, cut the engine and grab the vodka and Maglite from under the seat. I shut the door as soft as I can and go round back to the garden. The fog's lifted some, but thin clouds move in front of the full moon. The light waxes and wanes. I find where Sheila buried the Big Wheel, take a swig from the vodka and throw the cap as far as I can. No sense capping something you intend to finish.

I set the plastic liquor jug on the ground and shine the light on the loose earth, then set the Maglite down beside the jug so its beam shows where I'll need to dig. The shovel's stuck beside the loose dirt where Sheila left it, so I pull the blade free and set to work, plunging the spade in as far as it'll reach.

I sweat with each thrust and pull and heave. The night wind chills me where I'm wet, so I draw on the bottle for warmth. I get drunker the longer I dig. Each shovel of dirt seems less real than the one previous, like I'm dreaming this, like Sheila never buried the Big Wheel, like he isn't dead. The flashlight and the moonlight don't show much once I've got the hole started, so I work by feel.

After a third of what's left of the vodka, I feel the shovel hit plastic. I use the spade edge to brush dirt from around the Big Wheel until I can grab at the handlebar. I try to pull it out of the clay. This is harder than I thought, and my balance isn't the best it's been.

I wrench at the plastic bike, jerk it side to side and pull. I feel like the Big Wheel's coming loose, but the work's hard, and I sweat more than I done while I was digging. I cuss a bunch and kick at the damn thing, and I guess I make too much noise. About the time I've got the toy free enough to pull out of the hole, the sliding door opens off the kitchen. I know Sheila's standing there before I look at her or she says anything.

"Roscoe?" she says. "What are you doing?" She's in those inside-out gray sweats of hers with a bathrobe loose around them, no shoes or slippers.

I let go of the Big Wheel and toss the shovel blade-first into the pile of earth where it stands for a second pointed to heaven before falling. There's nothing I can say because she already seen what I'm up to.

"What the shit?" she says. "How dare you."

I wipe at the sweat with my hand and feel the dirt smear on my brow. "I'm cleaning up your mess," I tell her. "You had no right to destroy his things."

She's mad. For the first time in a long time, I've pushed her far enough. She comes off the porch barefoot and right up to me by the hole. "No right?" she says. "You sorry shit." She's yelling up a storm now, telling me about how he was her baby and she can do all she pleases and how I'm the one who's got no right to interfere. She calls me names—bastard, trash, s.o.b.

I yell back, and the shouting feels good. I tell her he was my son too, and that she can't just decide to bury all his stuff without me agreeing. The madder I get, the better I feel.

But then she changes. Her voice drops to a whisper and she looks away from me. "I never agreed to have him burnt up," she says.

I don't get it at first, so I tell her, "We made that decision together. You agreed with me."

She starts sobbing and falls down onto her butt, right there in the dirt. She's cried some since Riley passed, but never like this. She seemed to be holding something back when she cried before, but now she's blubbering and making these high-pitched sounds like a gut-shot hare. In the flashlight beam I can see snot and tears dripping off her face. This doesn't feel right anymore. I never could stand the sight of a crying woman, not my mother or my sisters, and not Sheila.

I feel like a jerk so I try to comfort her but she pushes me away, and when I try again to put my arms around her, she starts whaling on me with both fists, hitting me with anything she can anywhere she can reach, so I pull away quick. She's stopped that rabbit noise, but the tears are still coming and she's panting.

"Sheila," I say. "Stop it. Stand up and let's talk about this."

She doesn't, so I grab her by the arm and pull her to her feet, and she lets me.

"You're right," I tell her. No matter the argument, those two words were enough to end our fights because more often than not that's all she wanted me to say. I learned this soon after we married and never forgot it. "I had no right to dig up his Big Wheel. I was wrong."

Saying I was wrong usually ended it if saying she was right didn't. But tonight she looks at me like she's suspicious. Not that I can blame her, because I know I wasn't wrong.

"Look, go on back to bed. You're exhausted. I'll fill the hole back in."

"Liar," she says.

"I swear on my honor," I say. "I'll fill it all back in."

But still she doesn't believe me, so I make more promises, and she doesn't believe any of them either. We go around in circles, and I'm starting to get really angry, not in the good way like before, but maybe that's just the vodka wearing off.

Finally, I tell her, "You go on back to bed, and I swear on his memory I'll fill this hole back in. And in the morning when I get back from the mine, we'll scatter his ashes right here in the garden like you wanted."

She doesn't say anything, but seems to ponder whether she can trust me this time.

"Or," I say, "if it'll make you feel better, we'll bury him."

She starts to cry again, but not that dying animal crying like before, and I know I've almost convinced her.

"His ashes, the urn, all of it. We'll mark off part of the property and bury it all. Save up some money for a tombstone and everything."

"OK," she says. "That's all I wanted."

I take her hand and lead her back into the house and to our bed and tuck her in. I tell her I'll wake her when I get home and we'll make arrangements. She's so worn out she falls to sleep almost right away.

Outside, I pull the Big Wheel out of the hole and put it in the trunk of my car, then I fill the hole up as fast as I can because I'm scared she'll wake up again. If she sees the Big Wheel gone, she'll call me a liar. But all I promised was I'd fill in the hole I dug. I never said anything would be in the hole. I never lied. And this is too big a part of Riley to leave buried

*

I CRAB-WALK DOWN THE SLOPING SHAFT INTO THE ABANDONED mine with the flashlight held out in front of me and dragging the Big Wheel behind. If I go too far down this slope I'll run into the water that's pooled in the flooded out bottom. The waterline's gone up every time it's rained, and I've had to move my little altar to a new room a few times because I was scared the flood would take him from me.

I find the dug-out room. The Maglite's starting to run out of juice so the beam's faint and brown, but I know the room by feel. Along the edges of the back wall are all the G.I. Joes and Legos and stuffed bears that Sheila's buried and I've saved. Every night when I get so drunk that I can't stop feeling, that I can't stop hating everything that ever was or ever will be because none of it means a thing in damnation without him, I come down here and sit with what's left of him, and I let myself cry. Not like Sheila cried tonight. I don't know that I'm capable of that, but I let myself come as close to that as I can get.

Tonight I don't cry. I'm too tired, and my drunk wore off during the fight. I slide the Big Wheel against the back wall, clear a space for it among the smaller toys, and shine my light on all that's left. Most of the toys are still muddy from being buried in the garden, and some of the stuffed bears are waterlogged, and I know that I've failed him. He took such good care of all his possessions, and I've never been much at caring for anything.

In a few weeks, the company will blow the entrance to this mine shut, and all of this will be gone. I'll get moved to some other abandoned hole in the ground to keep the teenagers out. I've thought about moving my shrine, packing up all the relics and taking them to the next mine I guard, but Sheila's starting to make me question that. Maybe I should let them blow it all shut. Let him rest in peace down here in the dark. That's as good a tribute as any of us deserves.

THOSE
GIRLS

HER FIRST DRINK WAS STRAIGHT GIN. NEAT. HER PAPA WORKED
as a serviceman for a company that made mining equipment, and
he got sent all over the country to fix what broke down. One time
he came home from a trip with one of those small airline bottles of
gin, no more than a shot. Her parents were born again and seldom
kept alcohol in the house, but her father thought the small bottle was
novel, so he put it on top of the Frigidaire for a time when he felt in
the mood, or her mother did, or maybe they would split that one shot
of gin in two glasses with tonic and lime on Christmas Eve.

She was twelve. She watched him put the tiny bottle on top of
the Frigidaire while she sat at their kitchen table, so happy her Papa
was home. She decided to joke with her Papa. She and her Papa were
always joking. "The next time you leave me here on my own," she said,
"I'm going to climb on the counter and get that bottle of gin and I'm
going to drink it."

Her Papa stood up from the kitchen table, walked to the Frigidaire,
took down the gin, and sat back at the kitchen table without a word.
He held the small bottle in his hand and studied it. He set it down on
the table, then slid it across to her. "Drink," he said.

She looked at her mother, hoping for a way out of this joke. Her
mother hung her head and went back to the dishes.

"Go on," her Papa said. "Drink it. I want to see your face when you learn how alcohol tastes."

*

"MERRY CHRISTMAS," THE MAN SAYS.

She props herself on an elbow, lights a cigarette, and blows smoke straight ahead of her.

"Would you like me to stay?" the man says.

Her small apartment is only one room, two if you count the bathroom, but she doesn't count the bathroom. They'd fucked on the Hide-a-Bed. Next to them the small fake tree's lights blink on and off.

"It's late," she says, though she knows she won't sleep. She'll lie awake, clenching her fists in time to the slow blinking of the Christmas lights.

The man zips the fly on his khakis. He leans over and kisses her cheek because she doesn't turn to offer her lips. "I'll call you sometime."

"OK," she says. "Sure," she says. "Merry Christmas."

*

AT NIGHT HER NEIGHBORHOOD IN FEDERAL WAY GETS QUIET. HER one-room apartment perches above a garage detached from the house where the Roseliebs live. The Roseliebs rent her the room cheap. Their house sits on a cul-de-sac and the garage and apartment sit behind the house, away from the road. Behind her, nothing but forest. The quiet spooks her. The nights she sits alone all she can think about are the girls, the girls whose bodies keep turning up throughout King County, the dead girls, the nameless girls, the runaway girls discarded like spent gum or cigarette butts.

*

WHAT SHE REMEMBERS MOST FROM HER PAPA'S FUNERAL IS THE shoes they'd dressed him in. Shiny black leather shoes at the end of his casket. She was thirteen and she'd never seen Papa in black leather shoes. She'd never seen him in shoes that weren't dirty. That was half her life ago and she still pictures the shoes clearly.

*

SHE THOUGHT SHE WOULD MARRY ONCE, WHEN SHE WAS SEVENTEEN. She had just left home, left her mother and half-sisters and stepfather in that singlewide tucked up in the hollows around Black Bear Creek. She had left school, bought a Greyhound ticket, one way to Seattle, moved out with all she could fit in one small bag, and took the first job she could find, answering calls at the Kenworth plant. She was seventeen. He was thirty-five and a worker on the assembly line, and she was sure he would marry her. He told her he would marry her, but he was already married and his promises meant shit.

*

SHE LIES IN BED AND CLENCHES AND UNCLENCHES HER FISTS IN TIME with the blinking of the Christmas lights and she worries, worries about those girls discarded throughout King County, worries she could be one of them. She worries she's growing old. She worries about growing ugly as she watches the mirror. She worries about the damnation her mother told her awaits women like her.

*

WHEN SHE WAS IN SEVENTH GRADE SHE WOULD PLAY CHESS WITH A boy from school. She wasn't very good, but he was worse. One day the boy told her his pet lizard had babies. He asked her if she wanted a lizard when the babies got bigger. She wasn't allowed to have pets, and she knew her mother would never tolerate a reptile in the house, so she made it a home in a shoebox and hid her new pet under her bed.

She had no idea what to feed a lizard, so within a few days her mother found a dead lizard in a shoebox under her bed, and her mother took away her tape deck and all her cassettes to punish her, made her take all the posters down from her bedroom walls and burn them in the trash barrel out back, and made her begin private Bible studies with the pastor from their Holiness church. It would be in those meetings that a man first grabbed her breasts even though she barely had breasts. The pastor didn't seem to mind.

*

ANOTHER OLDER MAN SHE HAD DATED ONCE PUT HER IN A CHOKEHOLD. They'd come back to her garage apartment drunk from a party and as she stumbled toward the door she felt an arm around her throat from behind. She thought she was dead but she fought. She kicked, she scratched, she flailed until he dropped her gasping on the gravel driveway. The man had run back around to the driver's side of his van, then came running to her, pretending that it had been some other man who tried to strangle her, some other man who ran off into the cul-de-sac or perhaps the forest. He wanted to stay with her to protect her, then he pleaded with her not to call the police, and he tried to force his way into the apartment after her but she screamed and screamed until Mr. Roselieb came out and ran him off. She never saw him again, but sometimes at night, she would imagine his van turning slowly around the cul-de-sac. For a while, every set of headlights that swung onto her apartment were the headlights of his van.

*

SHE WORRIES SHE SHOULD BE MORE CAREFUL. SHE WORRIES SHE'S only ever said "I love you" when she's drinking. She worries she drinks too much, drinks alone too often, drinks with strange men too often. She worries.

*

WHEN SHE DRINKS SHE REMEMBERS HER PAPA, HIS SMILE, THE way his hands felt coarse and strong against her small hands. She remembers him taking her fishing, using lizards as bait as they waded into creeks and streams, the cold water churning around her waist.

She remembers the fish they caught, the way those fish tasted once Papa had gutted them and cleaned them and fried them with flour and lemon and light beer. She remembers the taste of those fish only when she's drinking. But when she sleeps, all she remembers is Papa's shiny black shoes, so she prefers to drink.

*

THE ATTACK LEFT HER BRUISED. SHE SWORE SHE WAS DONE DRINKING. She swore she was done with men. Men had never done anything she wanted to remember. She had learned shorthand and she had left the Kenworth plant for a better job doing transcription. She swore she would turn her life around, swore to swear off men and alcohol. But her promises also meant shit.

*

SHE DOESN'T REMEMBER HOW OLD SHE WAS THE TIME SHE STOLE her mother's powder and lipstick, smeared too much over her face as she looked in the mirror, then tangled her mother's curlers in her hair. She can't remember how old she was, not old enough to know what she was doing, but old enough to know she'd done it poorly. Still she wanted to show her Papa, wanted him to tell her how beautiful she looked, tell her she was beautiful the way he would tell her mother how beautiful she looked on those rare occasions her mother curled her hair and put on powder and lipstick.

But her Papa didn't tell her how beautiful she looked. He laughed and made her cry. He lifted her onto his chest and consoled her, called her "Papa's best girl" over and over, then dried her eyes, washed her face, tried and failed to remove the curlers without pulling her hair. She wouldn't cry even though he hurt her as he yanked the curlers out, she wouldn't let herself cry to protect him from the hurt he caused her, but after Papa put her to bed and kissed her goodnight and shut her bedroom door, she bawled as quietly as she could stand, clenching and unclenching her fists until her bedroom walls grew lighter with the rising sun.

THE DOG
YOU FEED

YOU CAN'T REMEMBER THE LAST TIME YOU THOUGHT ABOUT THE day Todd Haze drowned in the YMCA pool. Perhaps you forgot. More likely, you kept that memory like a chained dog you knew would snap its lead when it ground against something sharp.

This is your weekend with Jake, so you wait in the car idling in front of Marsh Fork Elementary. After the divorce, Ami moved in with a man she'd been screwing, an MSHA inspector named Don, and took Jake to live with him down in Black Bear Creek, a pimple on the asscrack of nowhere. This means you have to drive an hour to pick up Jake and another hour to take him back to Beckley, all on the two-lane Route 3, which winds along the Coal River and passes through one unincorporated town after another. Be glad you left the mines after the divorce and avoided ending up in some rusted-out trailer parked on a blind curve in some shithole like Dry Creek or Rock Creek or Naoma.

You got out of the mines but you can't escape them. Reminders rise from every direction in this valley. A coal silo towers above the school, a mere hundred and fifty feet behind the building where Jake spends five days every week breathing in the dust that scatters across the playground and works its way into the groundwater which then comes through the faucets and drinking fountains. Marsh Fork students miss more days due to illness than any school in West Virginia, maybe in the nation, and Jake has missed his share, most of them from unexplained stomachaches and migraines.

The dust that coats the playground can't be seen from this distance, but walk across the grass there and your shoes will stain black. But you can't walk across the playground. The area where Jake takes his recess every day is encircled by a high chain-link fence topped with razor wire like some *Vernichtungslager*. You're not sure whom the fence is supposed to keep out. Or worse, why they keep the children fenced in.

But the worst reminder of the mines is what can't be seen from the ground, the slurry dam topping the ridge four hundred feet above the school. The leaky dam is all that stands between the school and three billion gallons of toxic sludge. This is the life Ami has brought upon your son.

No, you can't escape the mines, just like you can't escape memory. No matter what you forget, memories find you over time.

The radio plays the Rolling Stones' "Shine a Light," but Brian Jones isn't what brings back the image of Todd floating facedown in the shallow end of the pool. The memory comes at the sight of a woman walking through the school's front doors with her hand around the back of Jake's neck. Not in a way that suggests she'll force Jake to do her will, but in a way that suggests comfort and guidance. The woman, her red pea coat and cream scarf swept against her in the January wind, brings back the memory. She doesn't remind you of Todd, not directly, but of Laura, Todd's sister, the first girl you loved.

*

Remember:

Third grade, watching Laura walk the perimeter of the Maxwell Hill Elementary playground by herself. She had friends, but she didn't play with anyone at recess. Her brown hair curled in rings to the point of her chin, except the bangs that curved up and out before they dropped to meet her brow. Sometimes another girl would walk beside her, but most of the time she walked alone, her hands in the pockets of her puffy pink coat.

No one had discovered girls yet, the softness of eyes and glisten of smiles. Games occupied the boys—the allure of rubber balls that could be thrown or hit or kicked. The girls' names were called last when picking sides, except for Christina, who could hit the back wall of the gym in kickball, or Summer, who was taller than all the boys and could guard anyone. Girls raced boys during the Presidential Physical Fitness tests and many of them won, but you didn't pay attention to the pale legs that stretched from those blue and gold shorts with each pulling stride. Laura wasn't particularly fast, couldn't catch or kick or shoot, so she was picked only when necessary and went unnoticed except those times she walked alone around the playground.

Then fourth grade when no one could help but notice her absence. Her father, Todd Sr., was blindsided when his heart stopped during Christmas pageant rehearsal at the United Methodist Church. Everyone's parents said he'd never had heart trouble before the cardiac arrest that killed him. Their whispers about Mr. Haze implied they were thinking the same could happen to any one of them.

Laura didn't come back to school before Christmas break. You thought that was it, she was gone. No one understood death, only its finality, and the finality for survivors. Their lives ended too. There was no returning from a parent's funeral, so no one expected to see Laura again.

But she came back after New Year's, and Mrs. Wickliff gave her the seat next to you, the classroom rearranged into rows of two-person tables so you couldn't hide from Laura. Death had made her exotic, her silence alluring and her eyes so bright with distance. Everyone wanted to say something comforting, but no one knew what. Mostly you wanted to ask what death was like, how it felt to go on living even though you had no right to.

One night you dreamt of her standing in the field beyond your grandmother's garden, the field abutting the treeline that sloped downward to the mouth of the gorge. In the dream Laura wore her puffy pink coat and stood with her hands in her pockets and the wind blew her hair to the side. She didn't see you. In the dream you loved her, so you woke loving her and kept loving her for months after although you didn't know what it meant to love someone and have that love returned.

You never figured out what to say to her other than to talk about classwork and slap bracelets. Sometimes she would whisper when the teacher was at the front of the classroom, but her words were never conspiratorial. The other boys called her your girlfriend with jokes and shoves during recess or in the bathroom. But she didn't know you loved her.

And then her brother drowned in April. Her mother pulled her out of school for good then, and they moved away, having lost all the men in their lives in a span of four months. One day someone belongs to a community and the next they do not, though you didn't understand this at the time, understood only the ideas of presence and absence, and never understood how Laura could flit between present and absent until she was gone.

*

In the shadow of the school's front door, Jake points to the car and the woman begins to lead him toward you. Something is wrong. Observe Jake's body language, the slouched shoulders and hanging chin that suggests defeat. Even though Ami left and took him away seven years ago, you've seen him in trouble enough times to recognize his physical reaction to the threat of punishment. Open the driverside door but leave the engine idling against the cold.

"Hey Dad," Jake says without eye contact. "I'll wait in the car."

When Jake has shut the passenger door behind him, the woman takes her right hand from the pocket of her red pea coat and reaches out. "Mr. Collison," she says. "I'm Ms. Petty. Jake's teacher."

Tell her to call you Jacob. Take her hand, thin and cold, and remember not to squeeze her fingers. Say: "What happened to Mrs. Shumaker?"

"Back surgery. I'm subbing the rest of the year."

You never liked Mrs. Shumaker. She was a rickety old bitch at parent-teacher in the fall. She seemed too old to deal with kids this young. Her back bent with a hunch above one shoulder and she had steely sideburns. "Jake is slower than the rest of the children in his class," she had said. "But you can't blame the boy. Children of divorce face a disadvantage."

Ms. Petty seems better already. Make her for twenty-three, twenty-four. She stands straight in what seems painfully perfect posture. Her hair is darkest brown, one shade lighter than black, and hangs almost to her shoulders, another three centimeters and the ends would touch her clavicle. This near miss bothers you. Her bangs slant off to the side from the part, and the wind pushes them flat against her brow. Something about her suggests she should be prettier than she is, though she isn't ugly, not even plain, just not as pretty as you thought she would be as she approached the car.

"Jake got in a fight today at recess," she says. "He busted the other boy's lip."

This is the first time you can remember Jake fighting. He always seems so gentle. Timid even. Ask who started the fight.

"Jake says the other boy started it."

Feel proud of Jake. Tell her she can't blame him. Tell her he should stick up for himself.

She will answer, "This is the third fight he's been in since I took the job."

Feel your pride wane. Try to think of an excuse; he's a good kid after all. Maybe there is a pattern of bullying and Jake is only sticking up for himself, or better yet, maybe he's sticking up for other kids being bullied. But this line of thought coupled with the three fights in such a short time frame suggests it's more likely Jake is the bully and you never knew it.

"I've talked with the principal and he agrees that Jake needs counseling for his anger. We want to schedule a meeting with you and your wife, on Monday if possible."

Raise your left hand and press the thumb to the back of the ring finger to show there is no ring. "Ex-wife. You probably want her new husband, they've got custody."

She looks away, turns her head so the wind sweeps her hair beyond her shoulder. What about her reminds you of Laura? Her hair and eyes are too dark, even her coat is not pink but red. Maybe the cock of her head or the wind at her face, like she was in that dreamt field behind the garden.

"I'm sorry." She sounds genuine. "I didn't realize."

Tell her it's an honest mistake. This isn't the first time people have assumed you're still married. The gesture toward your naked finger has become a stock response, a performance reserved for women, as though they need proof. Her left hand hasn't emerged from the pocket of her coat, so you can't check her finger for a ring.

"You should talk to Jake anyway," she says. "Maybe you can help him control his anger."

Jake has never been an angry child. Your half-brother Edom had been angry, had fought you every day growing up, was the first to throw punches or club with soup ladles. Even as adults you had your share of bloodshed. At your sister's wedding reception ten years gone, drunk on the bottle of gin you split, you gut-punched him and turned to walk away when Edom knocked you unconscious with a glass ashtray. But Jake, who has no siblings, not even stepbrothers or stepsisters, has never once fought another child to your knowledge, has never lashed out at inanimate objects or even thrown a nasty word toward his parents.

Say, "I'll do that," and the teacher will smile. Consider asking for her number, but she is too young and she would say no. There are probably rules against dating a student's parent. That's what you'll tell yourself, but recognize the truth even if you don't want to admit it: You've reached that age where being an older man is no longer exotic. Before, you could land younger women when you cared enough to try. Sure, they rejected you as often as not, but there was something fierce in those rejections, something carnal. Lately the rejections suggest pity.

Watch the teacher return to the school, the hem of her coat blown before her, and think of what a shitty job it must be to teach kids, to grow so close to them for a year and then lose them.

*

WONDER: HOW DID ANYONE LEARN FOR CERTAIN, THAT DAY IN school, that Todd had drowned during swim lessons at the YMCA? Try to remember. The teachers must have told you at some point; how else could it have been confirmed? There was never a mass announcement over the intercom. Remember the rumors that drifted into and around the classroom, that a boy had drowned, but you thought they were just that, rumors. Then Laura was called to the office, and you thought, no, not her brother, not so soon after her father. But she never came back, and everyone knew.

Think. Can you remember Mrs. Wickliff telling the class? Can you remember her crying? Not specifically, but that day everyone cried. The classrooms and hallways ran with tears. Even those people who never knew Todd, not directly at least, acted as though he were their brother. He was a quiet kid, not popular but not unpopular. He played on the basketball team, competed in Math Field Day, won the science fair. Maybe you sat near him on the bus. You know he never spoke to you. Still, you cried. Everyone did. Everyone lost him, everyone shared in that grief.

Coach Bradley, the gym teacher, took his death hardest. Under his supervision, Todd had drowned in the shallow end of the pool without anyone noticing until he was dead. In Coach Bradley's defense, Todd had an embolism or an aneurysm or something. There was little anyone could do—something that waited dormant inside him for eleven years had decided to burst and would've killed him on its own, but his lungs had filled with water before he died, and that made his death a drowning.

No one could have saved him. Still, Coach Bradley blamed himself. The day he returned to teaching, he had grown out his beard, and you were struck by how gray it was, how stark against the dark hair of his head, and how odd it looked on that always shaven face. Even now you associate beards with mourning. That first day back, Coach Bradley sat on the edge of the stage in the gym with the palms of his hands dug into his eye sockets. He sat doubled over. The class played dodge ball or kickball or something, but Coach Bradley didn't look up once. Everyone on the gym floor could have drowned and he wouldn't have noticed.

*

THINK ABOUT ALL OF THIS DURING THE DRIVE BACK TO BECKLEY because you want to avoid what Jake's teacher said about his anger. But then remember you have only fifteen weekends with him a year, not counting holidays. Only fifteen chances to parent him.

Jake has always been quiet around you, and every weekend he seems quieter still. So far he's been stone silent on the drive. He scans stations on the radio, looking for something he likes. Most of the stations have gone sports or talk radio lately, so there is little music. Jake settles on a country station with some girl whining about some boy who done her wrong so now she's going to smash out the headlights on his pickup. All it's missing is the hound dog. You can't abide the twangy pop that passes for country music these days, and you certainly can't abide some teenage girl singing about heartbreak like she knows anything about anything. Turn the radio off. Let Jake know you need to talk. Let him know you need to be heard.

He won't bring up the fight. You'll have to if you want to make progress this weekend.

Say: "Teacher told me you busted some boy's lip."

He won't respond to that simple bait. It isn't even a question. You have stated a fact obvious to both parties. He scratches at his eyebrow with the back of a fingernail and looks out the window.

Try again: "What happened?"

But that won't be enough either. Jake will shrug. Come at this from a different angle, be more specific. Start by asking what the boy's name is. Then ask what the boy did to get his lip busted.

"He mouthed off," Jake says.

Your impulse will be disbelief. "He mouthed off? Since when is it your job to bust every lip that mouths off?"

He will raise his voice slightly: "Since he started in about my daddy putting his daddy out of a job."

He has never raised his voice before and has never talked back. Now he has done both. Wonder who this boy is, who he thinks he is. He's not the child you remember from three weeks before. Wonder whose attitude this is. You want to blame Ami or Don, so blame them both before the meaning of his words occurs to you.

Try to think of what you did that could have put anyone else out of a job. During the summer, you work on a friend's landscape crew, digging holes and planting trees, and the rest of the year you clean professional buildings and office parks overnight.

Then realize he's talking about Don, Don the inspector who can shut down a mine for not venting its methane properly, or at least for having management who won't grease his palm. Don can put dozens of miners out of work with a single signature. Get angry that this other man has replaced you in your son's life. Think about turning the car around and driving back to Black Bear to give Ami a piece of your mind. Think about calling your lawyer and suing again. Think about getting redneck and challenging Don physically like you've always wanted to.

But none of those options seems feasible. Besides, you've never had trouble controlling your anger. You never fought anyone who didn't start the fight, and only then if you had an advantage. Self-preservation was always your first instinct. Fight when you don't have any other choice, duck when you can, and always take an opening.

Instead of revisiting those old battles with Ami, correct Jake: "Don's not your father."

Jake turns and looks at you for a second and turns away as fast. "Well, Samuel shouldn't of been mouthing off noways."

You don't want Jake to have anger problems, but know he's right about the other boy mouthing off. There's a time for fighting, and one of those times is taking up for kin. More than anything, knowing that he took up for Don tells you where you stand, what you stand to lose, and what you've already lost.

*

REMEMBER THE WAY IT FEELS TO LET ANGER WIN.

In that school of tears, there was one boy who didn't cry the day Todd drowned. Jamie Cottle was the principal's son, a spoiled sow of a boy a grade below who bullied everyone, older or younger. Every boy in the school harbored fantasies of beating the fire out of Jamie Cottle. But no one dared touch him. He ran the school through fear, making demands of everyone and threatening to tell elaborate lies to his father if anyone dared disobey his commands.

Jamie Cottle wore wire-framed glasses made for an adult because they were the only size that would fit around his head, but the lenses were too large for his sockets and accented his tiny squinted eyes. He had no athletic talent besides blocking off space, but he always made sure to be a team captain at recess. When he didn't make the school basketball team, his father started a J.V. squad and coached it himself.

The day of Todd's death, the teachers tried to go forward with lessons, but no one could pay attention, not even the teachers, so they gave an extra recess. You stood on the playground with the other boys, everyone holding a kickball or a basketball or a soccer ball, though no one could think of what to do with them. They seemed forgotten toys from a foreign civilization, like backgammon or Go.

Jamie Cottle came up to the circle. "One lousy kid dies," he said, "and everyone's going boo-hoo."

You never knew who threw the first ball at him, but everyone was pelting him with everything they had. The balls bounced off him and you picked them up and threw them again. He tried to run, but everyone ran after him, hitting him again and again. He fell over and you hit him. He cried and threatened as he tried to stand, tried to run, but no one listened. This was release.

The teachers didn't intervene that day.

*

CONTINUE TO FUME ABOUT HOW JAKE FEELS TOWARD DON AS YOU wind through Glen Daniels and come to the T-section of Routes 3 and 99. You want to prove you're Jake's father.

Tell him: "Teacher says this is the third fight you've been in here lately. Says you got problems controlling your anger."

Jake throws one hand in the air and then slams it down on his lap. You can't remember seeing this odd gesture before, from him or anyone else. Where did he learn this? He does it again: His left hand shoots up almost eye level and then he smacks it down against his thigh. He does it a third time.

Ask him what the shit he's doing. He stops smacking his thigh and begins to rub his palm against the same spot he'd just been swatting, as though he wants to rub away the imprint of this action.

"What does she know?" He rubs his thigh faster. "She's just a sub. She don't know me."

The voice isn't Jake's. His attitude seems learned, just like this strange gesture he's acquired. Some changeling rides shotgun in your car and you wonder where your son has gone. The body is Jake's, but he isn't the boy from three weeks ago. This means you have to reclaim your son, and to do that you must reclaim your role as father.

Think about what you can tell him. What can make him understand? What will leave an impression? Tell him you understand anger problems, you understand fighting. Tell him about how his uncle Edom had anger problems too. Tell him about all those fights the two of you got in from the time he was walking all the way through adulthood. The fights stopped only after Edom tried to swim the New River drunk on grain and got smashed against the rocks and never recovered from the cerebral hemorrhaging. Now he can't speak. He drinks through a tube down his throat and pisses in a bag. Leave that last part out. Leave out the accident all together. Jake's never known Edom, so why bother with all of this now.

Instead, explain that Edom's anger caused him problems in life. Problems keeping a job, problems with women, problems with drugs and alcohol. Realize you sound like an after-school special, but maybe you're getting through to him with this trite morality tale. Finish with fatherly wisdom, one of the fables granddaddy used to tell, the one about the two dogs.

Tell him: "You got two dogs that live inside you. One's this weak, timid mutt that gets itself kicked around, pisses itself soon as you raise your foot, and the other's this vicious dog, this pit bull or Rottweiler that'll take off your leg soon as you try and kick it. Know which dog gets bigger and takes over?"

Jake seems interested. He's looking at you now, keeping his eyes focused on your face, a first for today. "Which one?"

"The dog you feed."

Jake will sit back in his seat and look out the window, thinking it over, figuring it out. Feel proud because you made an impact on him. Look around at the scenery, the leafbare trees that patchwork the mountains on both sides, the muddy river seeming not to flow anymore but lie stagnant, the cinderblock outbuilding with "Scabs go home" spray-painted by an unsure hand.

You still have time to save Jake from all this.

*

REMEMBER THOSE SWIM LESSONS.

Every year, Coach Bradley took each grade to the YMCA the first week of April. They gave patches for how far people progressed during the week, and each patch corresponded to an aquatic species: Minnow, fish, flying fish, shark. You never progressed past guppy, the step above polliwog. Polliwogs used floatation devices. You got stuck at guppy because you couldn't master the freestyle, turning your head at the same time you swung your arm over and out. The other boys made fun, and you were angry, wanted to hurt someone, especially Edom who was two years younger but already a fish. Still, everyone looked forward to swim lessons because they disrupted your ordered life.

Remember fourth grade, April Fool's Day. You rode the bus to the YMCA and the sky was metallic with the threat of snow. Sean Lee wanted to play a prank on Coach Bradley. When Coach Bradley left the locker room so the boys could change into their suits, Sean slammed you against the lockers and started pretend punching. Several of the other boys were in on the gag and gathered around, chanting Fight!

Coach Bradley swung open the door, told everyone to knock it off and get dressed, then let the door slap shut. Everyone put their swimsuits on in quiet disbelief. But as soon as you reached the pool, as soon as you saw the steam collected on the glass windows and felt the chlorine sting your nose, everyone got rowdy again.

*

NOW REMEMBER WHAT YOU DON'T WANT TO ADMIT.

At the end of your lesson, the bus came to drop off the fifth graders and return the fourth graders to school. Everyone was dressed and ready to run to the bus with their wet hair freezing against their scalps when you realized you left your goggles on the bench beside the pool.

You've never told anyone you went back for your goggles, that you saw Todd floating facedown in the shallow end.

The lesson had not begun. The fifth graders were horsing in the water, and Coach Bradley scolded you for coming back in your streetclothes. He walked you to the stairs that climbed to the lobby. Maybe you were the reason he noticed Todd too late, but you saw him on your way out, his brown hair flowered out around his head as he floated on his stomach. Dead man's float. You thought he was playing.

Then later, when you heard the rumors that a boy had drowned, you knew what you had seen. You knew right away what this meant for Laura, and you wanted to protect her. Still, you didn't tell anyone.

*

FEEL ASHAMED, A QUARTER-CENTURY LATER, FOR MISTAKES MADE when you were Jake's age. Wonder how he would deal with this situation. Would he tell anyone what he saw, or lock it away to have it come back unbidden twenty-odd years later?

There's a machine parts company outside Beckley that spells out cute slogans on their marquee board. Few of these slogans have anything to do with machine parts, and most of them read like the aphorisms found in fortune cookies instead of actual fortunes. A few weeks back, the board read, "Memory is the mother of wisdom." Bullshit, you thought then, though you weren't entirely sure why. Now you know. Memory is a motherfucker.

You've never told anyone about Todd, but you think you should. Seek release. Unburden yourself to Jake. Tell him: "When I was your age, a boy drowned during one of our swim lessons."

Jake will look at you and wait for more. He will wonder why you're telling him this. You'll read the wonder in his silence.

Continue. "I saw him dead in the pool but didn't know what I seen. I thought he was playing so I didn't tell the teacher. I regret it like hell."

"Is this like the dog story?" Jake will ask, and you can tell he's trying to figure out what he's supposed to learn from your tale.

Answer him. "No, it's not like the dog story. This really happened."

Think about lighting up because your body needs nicotine to get through this. Anytime you feel strong emotion, you need a smoke to cope. You smoke when you're angry, when you're sad, when you're fit to be tied. But you've vowed not to smoke with Jake in the car. Not that it'll matter much since Ami smokes a pack a day and doesn't have the decency to step outside and away from Jake. This is one of the ways you make yourself feel like the better parent, so you'll resist the urge this time. Plus, you're almost home.

Wind up the mountain to Beckley, pass the city limit signs, and suddenly you're in civilization again. Pass the turn off to Tamarack ("The Best of West Virginia!" the nauseating orange and purple sign claims), and Harper Road stretches on in a run of chain restaurants and hotels. You have a theory that all the chain restaurants in Beckley have seating for a population twice the size of the city's, but you've never bothered to look up the numbers.

Know Jake will want to eat out tonight. He wants to eat out every weekend with you because there are no restaurants in Black Bear except the lunch counter at the back of the filling station. Plus, he says you can't cook, so you overpay for bad food in the theme restaurants he loves most. The weekends he stays in Beckley are like a vacation for him. But this time, you need to get through to him. This needs to be a lesson, a chance to bond in some meaningful way instead of the usual ignoring one another over chicken wings or fried trout.

Ask Jake if he's known anyone who died.

"Grandpa Corn," he will answer. Ami's father, Cornelius, died last year. You lost out on one of your weekends with Jake so he could go to the service.

"Were you sad when it happened?"

"Not really. I didn't like him. He smelled bad and his hands were hard. It hurt when he hugged me."

Tell him you hope it's a long time before someone he loves dies. Tell him nothing hurts more than death. Not for the person who dies, but for the people who don't. Because if you've learned anything, you've learned that death is something that happens to those who go on living.

Then look over at him. Really look. See him. His hair has grown a little too long in the back and his body is filling out around his bony frame. He has your mother's nose, that sharp angle that Edom inherited but you did not. This is your son. The body is his, even if the voice is changing and the words he has formed today don't sound like your boy. Still, this boy is Jake, and you look forward to these weekends with him throughout the three weeks that separate them.

"It's OK, Dad," he says. "You didn't never tell anyone about that boy who drowned because you were feeding the weak dog inside you. I won't do the same."

You fucked up. Granddaddy told you about the two dogs because he was trying to teach you to stick up for yourself, to fight back, not to be kicked around, or worse, tuck tail. The lesson you've just taught Jake is the exact opposite of the lesson intended. Remember Edom, all the stitches and broken bones, and think of those other fights you couldn't avoid when you were Jake's age, and all the fights you've avoided when you shouldn't have.

Feel like an idiot and wonder how you can undo your error without seeming an even bigger asshole. Give up as quickly. If you admit your foolishness, he will know you are a fool. He will grow up knowing your breed exactly.

THE MAYOR

for my parents

ETTA YORK'S HUSBAND CALLED THAT AFTERNOON TO WARN HER A power line had fallen across the road in front of Eccles Cementation. They were waiting for AEP to come repair the line, but that could be hours. In the meantime, his crew was warning motorists. Toby told her to be careful when she came to pick him up from work.

"It's a live wire," he said, "12,470 volts. So don't stop. Drive right over it."

She worried about that wire throughout the half-hour drive from Glen Morgan to Eccles to pick up Toby as she had done every afternoon for the past seven months. Hadn't she been told not to drive across a downed power line? She felt sure she learned that in driver's ed at Shady Spring High School. Toby was an electrician for United Mine Workers of America Construction, and she trusted he would never put her in danger. But still, she worried what 12,470 volts would do to her, and to the baby.

She came to the bottom of Harper Road, turned into Eccles, and saw the power line curved across the street like a copperhead waiting in the sun. On the opposite shoulder, sparks shot from the frayed end of the wire and flamed up in the brush. The line jumped. Toby said not to stop, but her instincts told her different. She braked.

She saw Toby waiting in front of the job site on the other side of the power line. He waved his hand toward himself, a sign to drive forward. He waved his hand faster as she came close to the wire. She popped the clutch and shifted the three-speed to second and punched the accelerator. She pressed her eyes closed and pushed the air from her lungs. She felt the front tires thud on the line. Then the rear tires.

She opened her eyes. Toby held out his hand, palm toward her, telling her to stop. She pulled onto the shoulder and wondered why he had not come to meet her on the other side of the downed line. She shifted into reverse and cut the engine. When she stepped out of the Jeep, Toby kissed her and put his hands on the edges of her belly. His beard scratched at her cheek.

"Why didn't you wait for me on the other side? Why did you make me drive across it?"

"Live wire." His eyebrows bushed together at his nose. "Didn't want to step near it."

"But you were fine having me go right over it."

"You were in the car. You were safe."

Her heart cadenced with fear and anger. The doctor had told her she needed to relax, mind her blood pressure. When her blood pressure peaked, so would the baby's. She drew deep breaths through her nostrils and held them, told herself to calm down.

"If you got out of the car near that wire, you'd have been in danger. You know I'd never want that." He grabbed her nose between his chapped knuckles like he might a child's. She forgave him despite her fear.

Toby helped her into the passenger seat, then took the wheel. He reversed the Jeep on the berm, pulled a U-turn in the street, and cut a wide arc across the centerline to avoid the live end. She closed her eyes again as both sets of tires bumped over the downed wire. She tasted blood in her mouth. She had been chewing the skin from her bottom lip.

"How was the doctor?"

"He said the Toxemia's back. I need to watch my blood pressure."

Every time she went for a checkup, she grew nervous, which she

knew accounted for her heightened blood pressure. She dreaded what
the doctor would tell her. Something could go wrong, or she could
lose the baby. She worried about spina bifida, anencephaly, cleft palate.
Blindness. Would she have the strength to love a blind child? She
prayed she would never learn if she had that strength.

She worried more about the delivery now that October was here
and the baby due at the end of the month. She had always trembled
at the thought of pain, and the pregnancy made that fear worse. Her
mother and older sisters told her she'd be fine, delivering a child was
nothing to fret about. But she would remain rooted in her fear until
she gave birth. The child would be their first. She married Toby a
year out of high school, but they waited five years to start a family.
At twenty-four, she still felt like a girl though she had a husband
and a house and, until recently, a job. Toby was nearly a year younger,
but he seemed older than she did, more responsible. He worked long
days, sent out their mortgage check on time, made repairs around the
house. He kept their lives upright.

"He say how bad it is?"

"The Toxemia? I'm to monitor my blood pressure, salt intake,
stress. I need to relax more. But nothing serious."

The doctor had told her she was nearing the borderline, that
if her blood pressure rose higher he'd have to perform a premature
C-section to avoid a stroke. She didn't want Toby to worry, so she
decided to withhold. He was concerned, she knew and respected that,
but his stress would only add to her worries.

She changed the subject, asked about his day at work.

"I got those bastards back," he said. He looked proud of himself,
his gloating child's smile and upturned chin. A few days before, the
guys on the construction crew had stolen his clothes and nailed his
boots to the floor while he showered. He told her about how he waited
until they were all under the showers, waited a few minutes until he
knew they were lathered up, then cut off the water from behind the
double-wide that had been converted into the bathhouse. "Other than
the foreman, I got the only key to the cage around the water heater
and fuse boxes, and the foreman already left for the day."

Laughing at his story made her muscles unclench. The UMW of A had been contracted for a new mine in Eccles, not far from the site of the 1914 explosion that killed more than 180 miners, including her great-uncle. Toby's crew was dropping four shafts and two slopes into the mountain, and his job as electrician was to keep the pumps, hoists, and other equipment running. The grunts thought he had an easy job, so they singled him out for pranks. She alone saw how worn down he was at the end of the day, saw the cuts and burns on his arms, his fingers mangled under heavy machinery. She knew how often he shocked himself and felt those pains with him. Her grandmother often said her empathy was her best trait and worst flaw.

Etta missed the regularity of a forty-hour workweek. She had kept her job as a receptionist until she was seven months pregnant and the fluid in her legs became too painful. Now they managed on one salary and one car between them, the CJ-7 hardtop with three-speed on the floor and a windshield that folded down. They had an International Harvester Scout, but the truck bled antifreeze and the engine block cracked during a February cold snap. So every morning Etta drove Toby to work, down Sullivan Hill and up Raleigh Hill, through the city of Beckley, and down to Eccles. Every evening she picked him up. These roundtrips ate away two hours of her day, but she didn't mind the drive. The hardtop Jeep made her feel safe, though she stayed cautious on the winding mountain roads.

Nausea had never been a problem. She gained less than thirty-five pounds of baby weight, and a lot of it in her face, legs, and butt, so her belly never got in the way of steering. The drive afforded her quiet time, which she knew she would miss when the baby came.

A Ronald Reagan campaign speech played on the Jeep's radio as they passed through Beckley. Reagan had been so handsome as the Gipper and Professor Boyd, and she trusted his voice. But the United Mine Workers endorsed Carter, so they would vote Carter. The UMW of A said Reagan would do away with unions, which meant Toby would lose his job. She worried what they would do, how they would survive, the three of them. If he couldn't find more construction work, he'd have to go into the mines. She had watched her grandfather die of black lung, his chest swollen and his back folded, watched him cough blood and tar onto his white handkerchiefs and bite at breaths he could not catch. She wouldn't let Toby do the same to their son. She slapped at the radio dial and silenced Reagan.

They came down the mountain above the town of Raleigh. Etta looked across at the shades of color, the red of oak and ash, yellow of hickory and birch, orange of maple and beech. She loved the autumn palette before November stripped every leaf brown. She was glad their son would be born in October and his birthdays would be decorated with the burning mountains. Her grandmother had taught her to identify trees by their leaves, where in the forest to find food, what could be eaten and what could not. "During the strikes," her grandmother told her, "we lived off what we could forage. You never know when another strike's coming and you'll be put out of your house." Etta knew how to survive on what the mountains provided and would teach her son the same.

They passed the Glen Morgan post office and the barbershop that stood in the hollow between two mountains. She would take the baby there for his first haircut. The barber would give him one of the lollipops in their bright primary colors and crisp cellophane. Toby insisted the baby would be a girl. He wanted to name her Tabitha after the daughter on Bewitched. But Etta knew he would be a boy, could feel the maleness inside her womb. She wanted to name him Woodrow Gulf after her father and her oldest brother, but Toby, who had no brothers and never knew his father, campaigned for Adam.

Toby turned the Jeep and began the climb up Sullivan Hill. He pointed out the window. "There he is," he said. "There's the Mayor."

She followed his pointing hand up the rise of Sullivan Hill to the large man on his stump. He was dressed against the October chill in a wool shirt checkered in blue and black, but he wore no hat. His gray hair curled around his temples, sat back from his forehead on a receded hairline. He had been there on her way down the mountain earlier, watching the traffic pass the post office and barbershop, but she had barely noticed him through her worry about that downed line.

She and Toby didn't know his name or anything about him, so they called him the Mayor of Glen Morgan. Glen Morgan had no mayor, just the post office and barbershop. Every morning when

Etta drove Toby to work, the Mayor would be sitting on his stump watching the cars drive down Sullivan Hill. Every afternoon when she left to pick up Toby, the Mayor would be sitting on his stump watching the cars drive up the hill. On summer days, he'd sit naked to the waist, his black breasts sagging against the girth of his belly. On winter mornings, he wore a fur-lined hunting cap and a wool pea coat, but still he sat on his stump. She had come to count on him, loved him for his reliability.

She asked Toby why he thought the Mayor was always there in the morning and evening, what he could watch for so many hours. She had asked these questions many times before, and every time Toby answered differently. The question and answer was a sort of private game.

"I bet he's retired," Toby said. "He's used to being up at a certain time and used to coming home at a certain time. Now that he doesn't work, he watches other people come and go. Old routines are stubborn. If I wasn't working, you'd probably find me on a stump somewhere."

"I know you. You'll never quit working, job or no job."

"You just wait. When I retire, I'll build me a sitting stump right there beside the Mayor, watch all those people go about their days."

She smiled at the thought of Toby sitting next to the Mayor, both of them shirtless in the sun. "Maybe he's watching for someone."

"Maybe he's waiting for a Missus Mayor."

"Maybe he's watching over us," she said as the Mayor faded from the rear window of the Jeep. "He's watching out for all of us."

*

ETTA TURNED ON THE TELEVISION WHILE TOBY LAY DOWN FOR A NAP after his shower. Most days he washed before he left work, but he had avoided the bathhouse since the incident with his clothes. Every day he napped. He would sleep for as long as an hour and a half if she let him, but those nights he was restless and kept her awake. She would wake him today after half an hour.

The television news showed the same Reagan speech they heard on the radio. "Let us base our decisions about peace and security," he said, "on the facts, on what we need to know and not on what we are told we must fear." The poll numbers between Carter and Reagan were almost even, everywhere except West Virginia and a handful of other states. She worried that Reagan would come down on the Mountain State, and the unions in particular, if he won.

She went to wake Toby. The blinds of their bedroom were drawn against the setting sun. The sun through the plastic blinds cast patterns on the carpet, and the room glowed a golden orange, a shade of orange she associated with death. The sky had shone that same golden orange the afternoon they found her little brother Jonathan stiff in his crib when she was ten.

She sat on the bed next to Toby. He was curled on his side atop the quilts, his knees bent around the pillow between them, his mouth hanging open. He looked so like a boy when he slept that way. Drool had caked at the corner of his mustache. The day she told him she was pregnant, he decided to grow a beard. She was still getting used to the sight of him with the trimmed blond hair covering his lower face. Somehow the beard made him look younger. She ran her fingertip across his eyelashes. He had such long lashes, longer and darker than hers even when she wore mascara. Women often stopped him to say how jealous they were of those lashes, then turned to her and offered a sympathetic smile, as though this erased their flirtation.

He blinked as her finger moved through the eyelashes. He pulled away from her, then sat up. "I thought I should wake you," she said. "So you don't sleep too long."

He scratched at the drool dried to his cheek. "I smell coffee," he said. His eyes were distant with sleep. "And cornbread?"

"Sure enough," she said. "I'm going to make some bacon and soup beans, and I found some greens down the hill this morning."

"Why don't you let me cook? Rest. Put your feet up."

"Cooking relaxes me."

Cooking did relax her. She enjoyed the hypnosis brought on by the repetitive stirs of the wooden spoon and the smells mingled above her grandmother's cast-iron skillet with its century of seasoning. She knew how to clean the skillet to maintain that seasoning, and she

never let Toby touch the pan. But more than relaxation, she hated
Toby's cooking. He meant well, bless his heart, but he shook in too
much salt, undercooked beans and overcooked greens.

"You can do the dishes," she said.

*

THAT SATURDAY SHE DROVE HER SISTER-IN-LAW, MACK, TO THE
dentist while Toby worked. He had taken on as many overtime shifts
as he could to help get their finances right before the baby came. She
sat in the dentist's sterile waiting room and chewed strips of skin from
her lip. Being that close to any doctor, no matter the type, made her
worry, even if she was not the patient.

When the dentist had finished Mack's filling, they walked to
the Burger Chef across the street from the strip mall of dentists' and
doctors' offices. The smell of fried grease made Etta's stomach feel
carved out. There was a line inside the restaurant and they waited to
place their order.

"I'm going to call Woody," Mack said. "Order me a shake?
Strawberry." She turned down a hallway toward the bathrooms and
the payphone bolted to the far wall.

Etta had two sisters but they were much older, and Mack was
more a sister to her than either of them had been. Her brother Woody
had come home one summer when he was nineteen and claimed to
have taken Mack for wife. She was fifteen, and Etta was thirteen,
the youngest of five after Jonathan's death. Their father didn't believe
their story, so Woody admitted they had never wed; they were waiting
until the girl turned sixteen. Mack slept on a cot in Etta's room the
rest of the year. This was the only time she shared a bedroom until she
married Toby.

Etta ordered a burger, fries, and two milkshakes from the girl at
the counter and carried the tray to a table in the back corner. A young
mother nursed a fussy infant a few tables over. The mother cooed at
him, said, "Hush now, Jonathan David." She began to sing. Something
about the woman's voice as she said the baby's name convinced Etta

that this woman loved this baby more than she had ever loved anything before him. Etta knew then that her own son had a name. She placed a hand to her belly and thought, "Jonathan David," which made the child seem more real and less frightening. She would tell Toby the good news when she picked him up that afternoon.

Mack looked pale when she came back to the table. She had been pale in the dentist's office, but now her skin looked as thin and translucent as butcher paper. "You look ill," Etta said. "Sit." Mack sat. Her eyes seemed unable to focus. "They were out of strawberry milkshake, so I got you chocolate," Etta said.

"We have to go to the hospital," Mack said.

"What's the matter? You don't look good." She thought Mack would faint. Maybe she was having a reaction to the local anesthesia. Etta hoped Mack would not faint because she didn't know if she could lift her sister-in-law into the Jeep.

"There's been an accident," Mack said.

"What happened? Is Woody OK?"

Mack's eyes seemed to regain their focus. "No," she said. "It's Toby."

*

SHE FOUND HIM ON THE FOURTH FLOOR OF THE HOSPITAL, LAID OUT on a gurney in the hallway. His head was swaddled in white bandages wound across both eyes. The bandages had stained red above his right eye. A sign attached to the gurney read, "Patient Blind" in bold lettering. She had to lean a hand against the wall when she saw it. She thought she would vomit or pass out. Her breaths came fast and short, and she couldn't seem to keep them long enough to draw oxygen. Her husband was blind.

"You're OK," Mack said. "Come now, I got you." Mack took her arm and tried to walk her the last two feet to the gurney, but still she could not breathe. She didn't want to move, but Mack pulled her along.

"Etta?" Toby said. He moved his head around despite the bandages.

"Here," she said. She laid her hand across his taut belly. "I'm here."

"Etta," he said and began to laugh. "I can't see." He laughed harder, guttural coughs that shook his shoulders.

A man in oily clothes rose from a chair near the gurney. She recognized him from the UMW of A crew, but she couldn't remember his name. She remembered having him and his wife over for dinner, remembered cooking them lasagna, remembered their son who brought little metal trucks with him and ramped them off the sofa in the living room while the adults ate in the kitchen.

"I'm real sorry," the man said. "I know he looks a mess, but he's going to be OK." He stopped talking and waited for her to say something. She tried to remember his name but could not. He seemed to understand her confusion. "Rudell," he said.

She remembered. His wife was Eleanor. She had picked at her food and did not compliment the cooking once. They never invited the couple over again, and the dinner was never reciprocated. "What's wrong with him?"

"His eye," Rudell said. "We were down to State Electric—"

"No." She cut him off. "Why is he laughing like that?"

"We waited here damn near two hours, blood pouring out of his eye, before they seen us. They wrapped him up and gave him some pain meds." Rudell picked at his nose with his thumbnail. "I guess they kicked in. I guess he feels pretty good."

"They made me take an eye test," Toby said. He laughed so hard he couldn't finish. The gurney rocked under him

"What? An eye test?"

"That damn male nurse," Rudell said, "he takes us back to this examining room, tells Toby to try to read the chart on the wall." Rudell started to laugh too. "There's blood shooting everywhere out of his eye, and the guy wants to know if he can see!"

Mack said, "Can you believe that?" under her breath. She dug around in her purse. Mack pulled out a rosary, wrapped the black beads in Toby's hand, let the silver crucifix dangle across his knuckles, and began Our Fathering in whispers.

Etta felt certain she would vomit. How would she take care of a baby and a blind husband? He wouldn't be able to help, couldn't change diapers or feed or carry the baby around when he woke in the night. Would he love a son he would never see?

"What happened?"

"We was down to State Electric to buy conduit," Rudell said. "Had it all loaded up in the truck, and Toby was trying to strap it down in the bed with a bungee. Hooked the bungee to one side of the truck and was pulling on the cord to stretch across the conduit. Had to yank to get it stretched, and the other end come loose. Hook got him square in the eye."

"Jesus Christ," she said. Mack said her Our Fathers louder at her swear, but Etta ignored her. "Just the one?" she said. "He hurt the one eye?"

"Sure," Rudell said. "But they had to wrap them both up, something about the pressure on his bad eye if they wrapped it but not the other."

"So he isn't blind? Not completely?" Her breaths drew out longer and the nausea settled in her gut.

"Far as I know."

A man in scrubs came down the hall toward them. She wondered if he was the same nurse or orderly who tried to get Toby to read the eye chart. "You the wife?" he said. He didn't wait for an answer. "We got a room open for him." The way he said this made her think he was talking about a hotel, last room in the inn, not a hospital.

"I better hit the road," Rudell said. "I still got that conduit in the truck, the boss is waiting on it. You let me know if he needs anything."

She thanked him for bringing her husband in and waiting with him, and Rudell left. The nurse pushed the gurney down the hall, and Mack stopped her prayers. Etta followed them toward the room. One of the gurney's front wheels had a hitch to its roll and turned sharp to the right every foot or two. The gurney smacked the wall and the nurse swore loudly. Toby laughed with every swerve.

Another nurse helped lift Toby from the gurney and into the bed. Etta thought the nurses seemed rougher than they should have been. They yanked him up by the shoulders and feet and plopped him on the bed like a feed sack. Toby moaned when he hit the bed and put his hand to the bandage above his eye.

The nurse said a doctor would be in soon, and Mack went to find a phone to call her husband. Etta pulled the chair to the bedside. She felt better when she sat, but she could still feel her heart beat in her temples. She no longer thought she would vomit, but she worried about her blood pressure. The poor child, she thought, poor Jonathan David. This must be hard on him, and he doesn't understand what is happening. She started to tell Toby the good news, the baby had a name, but she doubted he'd remember after the medication wore off.

Toby was quiet and his breaths came regular. She hoped he had fallen asleep. He was such a strong man. He had broken his nose during a company softball game, took a sharp grounder to the face on a bad hop, but did not quit playing. Blood had run down his chin. He came up to where she sat in the stands and asked for a tampon, broke the tampon in half and stuck one end up each nostril, then took his turn at bat. She drove him to the hospital when the game ended. Pain terrified her. She avoided physical hurt, revolved her life around this fear. But pain never slowed Toby down. She never expected to see him like this, in a hospital bed, loopy with medication and half blind.

The Mayor hadn't been there that morning when she drove down the mountain with Mack. She hadn't noticed at the time, but she was certain now that he had not been sitting on his stump, watching over them as she drove past. She couldn't remember another time he hadn't been there. Something had felt out of sorts, but she couldn't place what was missing from her day. Now she knew. The Mayor had not been there to watch out for them against dangers like these. The realization shook her.

She jumped at a knock on the door and turned, expecting to see a doctor. Instead she saw Ken, the pastor from the Assembly of God where they worshipped. She wondered how Ken knew Toby was here, how he heard about the accident. He looked solemn, the way a man of God was trained to look in this situation.

"How is he?"

"I think he's asleep. I don't know. I haven't talked to a doctor yet, so I don't know anything. They've got him drugged."

Pastor Ken walked over to the bed, placed his hand on Toby's arm. Toby raised his head off the pillow and said something incomprehensible.

"It's Pastor Ken," he said. "I'm going to pray over you, pray that God restore your sight. Trust in God. He heals all."

"That's right," Toby said. "I'm like that leper." He shook with laughter.

Pastor Ken smiled. Then he lifted the crucifix end of Mack's rosary, which was still wrapped in Toby's hand. His smile dropped off. "What do you have here?"

"I don't know," Toby said. "I got something in my eye."

*

THEY KEPT TOBY IN THE HOSPITAL OVER THE WEEKEND. THE HOOK had burst the lens of his eye. When the swelling subsided enough to operate, the doctors went in and sucked out the shattered lens. His pupil was paralyzed and he lost all sight in that eye. He could see pure white light, he said, could detect abrupt changes. That was all. No shadows, no forms, no movement. Only light, he said.

She drove him home after the third day. She had stayed in the hospital, eaten in the cafeteria, gone home to shower and sleep. Her spine felt like it would collapse with pain from sitting in that chair beside the bed for so long, dozing when Toby slept or refused to talk. He had been sullen. The doctors hoped they would be able to perform an implant and restore some sight to his eye, but until then he'd have to wear a black patch that made him look like a villain in a silent film.

She glanced at him as she drove them home. The nurse had shaved his beard before surgery, and two days' stubble marred his cheeks. Her sight was drawn to his bad eye. She didn't want to fixate on the patch, but she found herself looking at it. He had worn gauze taped over the eye for two days following the surgery, but the doctors replaced the gauze with the patch before he was discharged. She knew how the mutilated eye looked. His eyes had been clear blue, the first thing that attracted her to him, then his smile, then his muscular shoulders. Now his right eye was solid red with a dark purple cloud above the iris and pupil.

He sat quiet throughout the drive, turned the radio off as soon as she flipped it on. He put a cigarette to his lips.

"Please don't smoke in the car," she said. "The baby."

"I'll roll the window down," he said. He turned the crank, and the air inside the Jeep grew cold and loud.

"Still," she said. "Can't you wait till we get home?"

He drew a loud breath and threw the unlit cigarette out the window. He turned the window crank and the car became quiet again. She knew he was irritable after everything he had been through; she told herself not to take his behavior personally. But she wasn't used to him acting this way. She had seen him pout a few times before in the six years she had known him, but never for this long. She chewed her bottom lip bloody.

She wanted to talk about something, to get him to think about something other than his eye and how much money he lost every day he didn't work. The baby seemed a natural topic, but thoughts of the baby made her worry. Two weeks until she was due. She had felt Toby's pain so intensely through this process, had felt her own eye burst though it remained intact, that she worried the baby would also feel those sympathy pains, would be born with his father's red and purple eye and paralyzed pupil.

She hadn't told him the baby had a name. Every day in the hospital she wanted to tell him, but his mood never seemed right. His mood still seemed wrong, but she hoped the news would cheer him up, make him think about the future instead of the present.

"I forgot to tell you," she said. "I know what we should name our son."

"What makes you think the baby is a boy?"

"I know."

"You just know?"

"Yes," she said. She couldn't explain how she knew, and she didn't want to have this argument. "Don't you want to hear the name?"

"Sure. Go ahead."

"Jonathan David York."

"OK."

She expected him to say more. She wanted him to like the name, to share her excitement. "You don't like it?"

"Yeah. Sure. It's a good name."

"Why don't you like it?"

"I like it, OK? But I don't want to commit to a name until we know for sure." She wondered if he meant until they knew the baby was a boy or until they knew the baby would live long enough to have a name. "That was your brother's name," he said.

"His name was Jonathan Dennis."

"Still. You don't think it's bad luck to name our son after a baby who died? You're the superstitious one."

She considered telling him she got the name not from her brother, but instead from the baby in the Burger Chef, and the similarity was coincidence. This sounded ridiculous when she thought about putting it into words, and she knew how he'd react. She could see his point. The name would be bad luck.

"You're right," she said. "We'll think of a different name."

"Like Tabitha," he said. In her periphery, she saw him smile for the first time since the pain medication wore off. She couldn't tell if he meant the name as a joke or if he was serious. "But you're probably right," he said. "We're going to have a son."

She felt his mood lighten. His presence seemed to relax, and he placed his hand on her thigh. But she had grown unsettled. Her breaths came fast and shallow and she felt dizzy. She focused on the red and orange and yellow trees on the mountainsides and told herself to calm down, this was no time to hyperventilate. She watched the trees pass the windshield and took deep breaths and willed her muscles to relax. She turned the Jeep onto Sullivan Road and began to climb the mountain toward home.

"Look," Toby said. He leaned down and reached to point across her. "There's the Mayor."

The Mayor's reliability didn't make her feel better, even if she knew she could count on his presence. For the past several days, the baby inside her had a name, which made him a person. But now the child was nameless again, and she doubted everything she had convinced herself of. In two weeks she would feel pain like she had never felt, and the chance remained that something would go wrong, that she would lose everything. Toby's eye had shown her that accidents were possible, that bigger accidents waited.

She could not look long enough to see the Mayor well, could make out little but his form on the stump and the blue of his checked shirt as they drove past, but she would swear she saw his head turn to follow their Jeep up the hill.

RIVER LIKE IRON AND MUD

THE WATER SMELLED OF IRON OR COPPER. THE BANKS SMELLED OF
fish, but the river always of metal. Parker tried to keep his mouth
shut against the river because he knew the water would taste of ore.
He sank so his eyes peered above the water's surface, like hippos he
had seen on nature programs, and watched the other bodies—his
girlfriend, Maddy, and two of her friends, Jimmy and Desiree—move
through the calm green river.

They swam in a chin-deep pool in the Coal River below the
ruins of the old gristmill that stood on the far bank opposite Black
Bear. They had waded across the river on Pack Mule Ford, a strip of
shallows the Shawnee had used as part of the highways their war and
hunting parties left crisscrossing the river valley, half a mile downriver
from the trestle bridge that seemed to sound its death rattle with
every loaded-down coal train that clattered across.

They had all stripped their jeans before taking to the ford, slung
denim across their shoulders as they walked across in T-shirts, and
tossed the jeans on the bank shadowed by two walls of the gristmill
that had not yet fallen into the river. The rear wall stood complete,
its red bricks still clinging together with perfectly square holes
where windows had been. The second floor windows left swatches

of sunlight in the shadows cast on the ground, and through the holes Parker could see green leaves stretching up the slope of Coal River Mountain behind. The south wall hadn't fared as well. A quarter of the original brick stretched up to meet the rear wall, but the one remaining window had collapsed and all the brick above had scattered to the world.

They had waded out into the pool of calm, shaded waters where they swam and floated and climbed on one another's backs. The other couple, Jimmy and Desiree, had stripped to their underwear, and Maddy had done the same, but Parker left his shirt on because he was embarrassed about his belly, and the cotton clung to his chest and gut as he sank in green-brown water to his chin.

Parker was a month shy of thirty. Maddy and Jimmy were both nineteen or twenty, he had trouble keeping it straight. He didn't know Desiree's age, but she could have been younger yet. Maybe even still in high school. They were Maddy's friends and they made him feel old. Before he got mixed up with Maddy, he thought dating a teenager would make him feel younger, but she made him feel sadder and older and lonelier than he had felt before she moved out of her parents' trailer in Sundial and into his prefab house deep in the hollow of Black Bear Creek.

As sad and lonely as he felt with Maddy, he still felt better than he had when his ex-wife left him with the mortgage six years before. He had started smoking and drinking when she left, had stopped eating regular meals, lived days at a time on cigarettes, coffee, and bottom-shelf rum. He had exercised regularly through high school, had carved his body into lean muscle, but the salad years of his marriage had seen him put on a layer of fat. Post-divorce, his starvation-fueled body ate away fat stores and began to chew into muscle, leaving him hollowed and hard. His metabolism slowed to a slouch.

His metabolism never sped up again when he quit smoking, and he put on thirty pounds like he might shrug on a coat, but he couldn't lose the pounds as easily. Not that he tried. He wanted to slim down again—he hated to see himself in the mirror, his gut beginning to distend and his chest sagging into breasts where before he had solid but never bulky pectorals. But want to lose weight as much as he might, he never did anything to make it happen, never jogged or went to a gym like people in the city did. There were no gyms in Black Bear. Besides, he sweated enough patching potholes with stinking tar for the State Road Commission, so the last thing on his mind at the end of the day was sweating more.

Maddy did little around the house, never cleaned or dusted or folded laundry, but she did cook, and she made sure he ate what she fed him, so before he knew better he had put on another twenty pounds and was too embarrassed to stand in front of the mirror without a shirt, let alone in front of three teenagers in their underwear. Maddy told him his gut wasn't as big as he let on. She accused him of puffing out his belly when he complained of feeling fat. Sure, she said, he had extra baggage, but she found pot-bellies sexy. One thing about Maddy, she couldn't lie for a damn, but he was glad when she tried for his sake.

He watched Maddy and her friends horseplay in the river, and he floated with his eyes just above the surface until he snorted water up his nose. The metallic water burned his nostrils and throat, and he felt its chill in his eye socket. He climbed out of the river and shook like a bear might. His soaked T-shirt sucked tight to his belly, and he regretted his choice. He was too embarrassed to go shirtless, but he never expected how much more ashamed he'd feel with wet cotton clinging to his gut. He pulled his legs into jeans and slid to a crouch against the gristmill's rear wall, his fly unsnapped and his feet bare, and he studied the kids in the water.

The guys on the State Road thought he was living a dream, coming home to a teenage girl every day, but he never dreamed this life. He enjoyed her company, and he felt lucky, but every day he expected her to leave. Every day he was surprised this thing with Maddy had lasted as long as it had. He waited for her to be packed and gone one day when he came home from work. These expectations were not fears, he told himself. He wasn't scared to lose her. That she would leave seemed inevitable, a fate he saw no choice but to be resigned to because there was no alternative, but then again, he never pictured his ex-wife leaving until she did, and even then he couldn't admit that she was gone.

"One day when I get out of this holler," Maddy said often. The clause that followed was changeable, though she had several she favored. Sometimes she claimed she would find a rich man and give him children in exchange for a comfortable life. Sometimes she would become a hairdresser. Sometimes she'd drive west and keep driving and never look back. Sometimes she'd move to a place where it was warm year round, and the water smelled of salt, and all the people were tan. "A place like Myrtle Beach," she would say, having gone there for her grandparents' fortieth anniversary when she was twelve.

Most often, she said she'd go to college and become a nurse. There was a school in Beckley, just a half hour up Route 3 from Black Bear, and they had a nursing program, and there were two hospitals in the city, but Parker doubted Maddy would ever make it that far. He expected her to leave him, but not to leave the valley. Few people made it out of the hollow they were bred in, and those that did never talked about leaving; they just left and never came back. Maddy still worked the same job she had in high school, filling coffee mugs at Guy's lunch counter, a high school job full of high school girls. High school girls and Maddy, who never left. Maddy was the type that talked.

If she left him, he didn't know where she would go. Her parents had made it clear there was no coming home. He wondered if she stayed because she had nowhere else to go, or just nowhere better. He couldn't bring himself to believe she stayed because she wanted to.

Maddy and the others waded out of the river, the girls twisting and squeezing the water out of their hair to leave puddles on the mud bank. Jimmy lit a cigarette and pulled deep. He had a tattoo above his left nipple, a skeleton peeling back Jimmy's flesh to grin, knowingly, at Parker. Maddy eyed his cigarette, and Parker knew she didn't light one too only because he was there. He smelled cigarettes on her most days when he came home from work, or after she had been out with friends. But she was too considerate, or too afraid of how he'd react, to smoke in front of him.

Desiree talked about something, a story involving two people Parker didn't know. Her story didn't sound interesting, but she kept talking as she rummaged the pile of clothes for her jeans and top.

"So they pull in at the cut," Desiree went on. "Not the cut over by Rock Creek, the one at Dry Creek. There's a bunch of hillbillies tailgating over there. You know, the usual. Tommy gets out of the truck asking if anyone's seen Dino, but sure enough no one knows anything about where Dino is, no one's seen him. He's been running his mouth all week about Tommy this and Tommy that, but when Tommy shows up, no one's heard a word from Dino."

Maddy and Jimmy weren't paying mind to her story either. They seemed too busy studying one another to hear the saga of Tommy and Dino. Parker watched them look at each other and watched each catch the other looking. There was no embarrassment in those looks, no coy turns of face or eyes, yet there was nothing predatory either, no urgency. They looked on one another's bodies like people familiar with what they saw.

Jimmy broke their commerce as Desiree stood with her clothes in hand and moved toward them, her jaws still spinning out her tale. Maddy turned toward Parker and smiled what he took to be a smile of embarrassment. He knew what he had not realized before—she had a place to go when she left him. He felt something akin to sorrow, something akin to relief.

A slight itch or burn began around his right ankle, then gained speed and purchase as it spread up his leg toward his knee. He swatted at his calf, and the burning turned to repeated stings from ankle to knee, and the stinging grew harder as he scratched, then began on the left ankle too. He stood and stomped his feet and kept scratching and the stings continued.

"Parker," Maddy said. "What the hell?"

Hundreds of fire ants, their red and black bodies pouring out of a small burrowed hole near where he had been sitting, swarmed his feet and ankles and up into his jeans and back out. He swatted at the legs of his jeans, but they did not stop or fall out but bit and bit, and he felt each distinct bite through the general haze of pain.

Jimmy grabbed his arm and jerked and pulled Parker after him toward the river. Parker fought against him, tried to pull away and tried to free his arms to keep swatting at his legs, but Jimmy held both his arms and dragged him farther down the bank. Jimmy had become a part of the larger struggle, an enemy in league against him. Parker lost his footing on the slick bank and was pulled into the river headfirst. The water was cool and tasted of old pipes. As Jimmy stood him on his feet in the muddy river bottom, the stings lessened, lessened, and stopped.

*

When they stripped off his jeans, small red bumps ran from his ankle to his knee, covering all but a few inches of flesh. The others wanted to drive him to a hospital, but the nearest was in Beckley.

"No," he said. "Take me home."

Jimmy insisted he needed a doctor. "Shit, man," he said. "They look bad. Shit."

"I'm fine. Really. Take me home," Parker said. "Just, let's hurry."

Maddy helped him into the house and got his clothes off before dumping him in the tub. They ran warm water and washed his legs, but the bites burned just as much as they did before the washing. She toweled him dry and helped him rub hydrocortisone cream on the bites to stop the itching. The itching didn't stop even with the cream, only dulled. Maddy helped him onto the couch, and they stacked pillows under his leg so it was propped.

When she asked if there was anything she could bring him, he asked for whiskey. "And fetch me a belt. The canvas one."

He took a drink of whiskey from the bottle and the burn felt good—a burn he could cause rather than be victim to. His head felt drunk and funny as things were, so he figured the whiskey couldn't hurt. Maddy helped him wrap the belt around his thigh just above the knee and thread the canvas strap through the buckle. The poison was spread through his blood, this he knew, but he hoped the belt would slow the course. He pulled tight, and the belt cut into his flesh.

Even with the cream, his leg itched. He fought against scratching but could go no longer than a minute or two before he had to give in, no matter how Maddy scolded. He tried rubbing with the flat of his hand rather than attack the welts with his fingernail, and rubbing helped some, but nothing stopped the burning.

"Like a thousand wasps," he kept saying. "Those damn ants bite like wasps."

After time and whiskey, he lost consciousness. When he came to he was in their bed, his leg propped and Maddy lying beside him, her hand on his chest. He lay close to the wall. Through the window blinds, blue light flickered. He had installed a light at the top of a utility pole on the edge of the property, one of those streetlamps with a sensor that turned the lamp on when the sun set. He bought the lamp at a home improvement store and climbed the pole to hang the light so it shone on the gravel road and part of his property. The bulb was one of those halogen numbers that shone blue-white, but there was a short in the wiring, so the light flickered like the bug zappers that hung from the trees around his parents' house further up the hollow.

He tried to sit up to scratch his leg, but his body felt stiff and sore, almost immovable. He rocked up a few times but never close enough to the leg. His movements woke Maddy.

"What is it, baby. You all right?"

"My leg itches."

She placed her hand on his chest and pressed him back onto the mattress.

"You best not scratch at those," she said, "only make matters worse. Settle, and I'll get you some more itch cream."

He sat and scratched as soon as she was out of the room and the itch felt some better, but not all better. Fever had grabbed him, he knew. His head was fuzzy and his skin clammy. His body was fighting off the poison in his blood, or else those bites were beginning to infect, or maybe both, he didn't know. The flicker of the blue streetlamp made everything seem less real.

Her shadow stood black in the doorway and moved toward him like a reckoning. She was there at the bed again. Her hands felt cold on his leg, or they felt normal and his leg was burning. She daubed the cream on each bite, slow and methodical. He didn't want her to leave.

"I love you," he said.

"Shut up." She pressed the back of her hand to his brow. "Yep," she said. "You got a fever."

"I know," he said. "But still. I mean it."

"Mmm," she said. "Right."

This confirmed his fears. She loved Jimmy. She would leave him, was there now only because she pitied for him. He felt like crying but knew if a man cried in front of a woman once, she would never respect him again. Besides, he thought, it was the fever crying, and not him.

"What is it?" She set the cream on the nightstand and lay back beside him. She stretched her arm across his chest and held her hand so the fingers with cream on them wouldn't touch him. "What's the matter?"

From his ex-wife he had learned never to talk about his problems. A man revealing his burdens to a woman led to naught but trouble. But the fever shook him and told him to give in to fear.

"I know you're screwing Jimmy," he said.

"You're crazy," she said. "You lost your damn mind."

"I saw the way you looked at each other," he said, "like you'd seen each other naked before."

She was quiet for a time. He couldn't say how long her silence lasted. Could have been no more than a minute, more likely nothing but a few seconds, but the hum from the air-conditioning seemed to stretch on an endless loop.

"Jimmy and I used to fool around some back in high school," she said. "But we never did it. Just teenage stuff. Hasn't been nothing since then, I promise you."

He wanted to believe her. She had confessed to more than she could have gotten away with. But he couldn't let himself believe because to do so would mean to unbelieve what he had been so certain of.

"Shit," she said. "I love you, stupid." She pulled her arm back and wiped her hand on her nightshirt, then reached across his chest and squeezed him. "But I know you don't love me. I known all along you don't, but I keep fooling myself."

"I do love you."

"Right," she said. "Your lips may be moving, but I know it's that fever talking."

The streetlamp went out and dropped the room in blackness. The thermostat clicked in the hallway, and the air-conditioner hum grew louder for two seconds before the air kicked on. The cool felt good on his leg and relieved the burning some. He could smell Maddy's shampoo when she moved her head into his neck, but she still smelled like the river, like mud and iron, underneath all the shower smells. The light flicked on again outside.

"I don't know," he said. "Maybe I love you now. Maybe I was too scared to before."

"But you're not too scared now."

"No," he said. He doubted she believed him, but he saw the lie to its completion. "Ain't scared of a thing right at this moment."

*

By morning the bites had grown infected. Parker knew before he had even seem them because of the way the itch had turned to pure burn. Bright red haloes circled each bump, and the bites themselves were swollen and yellow-white with pus.

"Good Christ," Maddy said. "Let's get you to the hospital."

"No doctor," he said. "We'll drain the pus, and everything will be right."

She touched his leg with the tips of her fingers like she was scared the bites would burn her. "I don't know," she said. "You need antibiotics."

"I know what I need, and I don't need to go to some doctor who's going to charge me a fortune just to drain out the infection, when I can do that my own self."

She pulled her hand back from his leg and turned away from him.

"Look," he said. "You want to be a help? Go put some coffee on."

She stomped as she left the bedroom and even on the thick carpet her steps echoed. He lay on the mattress with his hands over his face until he heard the Mr. Coffee in the kitchen start to gurgle and smelled the steam and grounds. He remembered what he had said the night before, what had come out of his mouth when he had lost his self-control and let the fever and the fear do the talking for him, and he was embarrassed. If he pretended the conversation never happened, he hoped, maybe she'd pretend the same and things could keep going as they always had before. He'd pretend he had never caught her looking at Jimmy the way she had, and he'd continue to pretend she didn't reek of smoke every time she came home from spending time with Jimmy, and maybe she would pretend he never said any of the things he had said, and they would keep living that comfortable life for as long as the mutual lies could be sustained.

His leg felt stiff when he stood but he managed to stumble into the bathroom. He pissed a steady but weakened stream into the toilet and then began to rummage through the cabinets and drawers until he found his grandfather's old safety razor in the tattered blue box the razor had come in, with "Murphy's Department Store, Beckley, W. Va." embossed in gold on the underside of the lid. Murphy's had shut its doors long ago with most of the old businesses along the brick streets of downtown Beckley, so the razor seemed a testament to how life had been for his grandfather, those times that he imagined were simpler and happier than the life he knew. He popped open the razor and pulled out one of the blades. The blade was rusted through the middle, but the edge looked clean for the most part.

He grabbed the bottle of rubbing alcohol and some cotton balls out of the medicine cabinet, and scooped up the whiskey bottle from the coffee table as he passed through the living room. He deposited his goods on the Formica dining table in the kitchen and dropped into one of the folding chairs. Maddy poured the coffee into mugs. He knew hers would be blonde with the expensive flavored creamers she loved, and his black, the only way he took coffee.

"Fetch me a lighter," he said.

She rummaged in a drawer before she set the mug of coffee and a white plastic Bic on the table in front of him. "What's all this," she said.

"Well, the whiskey's for me." He poured a shot into his coffee but left the lid on the table. "The rest is for my leg."

"You can't be serious," she said.

He began to heat the razorblade by passing its edge through the lighter flame.

"Stupid ass," she said. "If you're going to do this, don't do it here. We eat here."

She helped him carry all the gear and a chair into the bathroom. They set the chair on the tile beside the long counter where everything would be within reach. Together they rubbed alcohol up and down his legs to make sure all of the bites were covered. He passed the razorblade through the flame until it was good and hot, then poured alcohol on the blade. He took a sip of his coffee, then another straight from the whiskey bottle.

"Fetch me a rag," he said. As she left he pressed the blade across the bite closest to his knee, then turned the blade horizontal and cut a cross into the bite. The cuts burned, but not in the way the bites had burned. The sting was more direct and solitary, not as general as the swarm of ants had been, and he felt he could control the pain, which made him feel powerful and not helpless as he had the day before. He put his fingers on either side of the bite and pulled open. Pus drained out. He continued to spread the wound until the blister ran red with blood.

Maddy came back to hand him the washrag but pulled up short. The pus and blood ran down his calf as he began to cut open the next bite. "Shit," she said. She turned her head away from him and shook the rag in his face.

He drained the second bite until it bled, then took the rag from her. "Thanks," he said and began to wipe the pus and blood from his calf.

She turned all the way from him, then turned back as he sliced open the third bite. As he wiped away the secretions she stumbled into the hallway and started to gag. "I can't watch this," she said.

"Suit yourself," he said. He sliced into the next bite. "You're the one who wants to be a nurse."

By now the pain had begun to lessen, his leg numbing with each pass of the razor blade. He heard her run down the hall and heave in the kitchen, though it didn't sound as though she got anything up. He didn't understand why, but he blamed her for all of this, for the bites and for what he was forced to do to fix the problem, and most of all for his weakness last night. She had created the situation that he was forced to deal with, so he wanted to make her aware that she was the cause, to punish her.

She had returned to the doorway by the time he sliced open the seventh bite. "I can't be here," she said. "I can't be in this house knowing you're in here doing this. I have to leave."

"That's fine." He made the cross cut and began to pry the fluid out. "See you later."

"Stupid ass," she said as she let the door slam behind her.

He knew she would smoke cigarettes wherever she was going. She would come home smelling of smoke, yet still lie about having smoked. More than the fact she'd sneak around like that, the lies bothered him. The taste and smell of cigarettes was so obvious under her mouthwash and perfume, he'd know she was smoking even if he had never touched a cigarette in his life. She took him for a fool, and that was what hurt. But he had never called her out on these lies, not really, so maybe he was a fool.

He knew she was screwing Jimmy. No matter what she said the night before, he knew what she was up to. He drank from the bottle and the bottom-shelf whiskey stung. He knew the code, knew this meant he should kick Jimmy's face in. Had he been ten years younger, he would've gone and done it just as soon as he quit cutting himself open. Whether she was cheating or not, Jimmy deserved a beating for the way Parker felt. But more than anything he felt too old to fight over some girl, even if she was his by all rights. Besides, he thought Jimmy would have a jump on him.

He took another swig on the whiskey and cut open another bite, turned the blade and sliced a second slit across the first, motions he had repeated so often that he no longer felt each cut.

AUGURY

Ardieth had almost finished undercutting the face when the carbide burned out and his place went black. Thirteen years in the mines and his breath still stopped at the utter dark that rolled on and on into the mountain, darkness stretched formless and infinite to hell and back, though he felt the walls and floor and ceiling press in on him, the overburden hung there to bury him. His movements in the dark were not movements because he could not see them.

Carbide burned four hours, his only means of keeping time. Three or four carbides a day, eight to ten tons cut and loaded and carted to the drift mouth, twenty-five cents a ton. Murmurs from the Union had passed through the Black Bear camp, talk of pouring out the water, but the darkness said no one was there but him and this was all he could do, keep cutting and loading. The darkness told him he had spent nearly four hours picking away at the kerf and fitting the sprag to hold up the undercut. The darkness told him he had lost speed. Twenty-five years old and his body already slowing down.

He felt for the headlamp and unclipped it from his hat of soft leather. The metal was hot to his touch. He unscrewed the bottom of the headlamp and felt around the place for his lunch pail. In the top section of the pail, where Karina used to put the pies she baked him, he kept spare carbide. He fingered the carbide in the dark, packed it in the bottom of the lamp, and touched the floor near the wall to find water. Water was never difficult to find, puddled as it was on the floors and along the walls, dripping from the shale roof. He filled the lamp with water and let a few drops slip into the carbide and heard the gas sizzle. He fitted the bottom to the lamp and screwed the two halves together. The light would come soon or it would never come, a panic as familiar as the damp in his lungs. He pressed his palm to the scorched lens and held it there, the lens burning into his skin, and felt the suction form.

He slapped his palm away from the lens and the suction ruptured. Light burst from the headlamp as the wick lit and the little flame leapt from the reflector. His canary in the wooden cage turned her head toward the sudden light but did not make a sound. The light shone black against the coalface as he fitted the lamp to his hat and took up the pick where it lay in the coal and slag from the undercut. With the light he could breathe, though he saw how small, how compressed the world had become. He struck the pick against the kerf and dug the undercut deeper so the coal would fall away clean when he shot the face.

His palms ached against the pick. Karina had rubbed his hands those nights he came home to her, rubbed his knees and back, then they had made love, the dust still coating his body rubbed off on her and the sheets she kept so clean.

He took up the breast auger when the undercut was deep enough and wide enough for the face to fall away with the shot. The steel auger was as tall as he was, too tall to stand full up in the low coal. He fit the plate to his chest and the drill end to the face at the correct angle and began to turn the crank. The bit ate into coal. Dust scuttled down and stung his eyes as he drilled the auger upward into the face. That first night he came home to her after bringing her back from Puerto Rico, Karina had cried over the ripped blisters on his hands and the blood mixed with coal dust that coated his skin a purple darker than death. She made him buy gloves with his next paycheck, though it meant they couldn't afford enough meat for her to eat. She ate bread and eggs, watched him chew pork with his beans. Holes had eaten through the gloves after she passed and he never bought another pair. He let the blood go, let it run into his cuffs and down his arms, as he cranked the auger.

He pulled the auger from the face and stuffed the hole with blasting powder. Those first years in the mines, when he was still a child, the powder had unsettled him because he knew how close to death he was each time he handled the volatile fuel. But now he welcomed the risk as he stuffed the powder deep, deep into the hole and corked it with clay. He pushed on the clay with the tamping rod and needle and felt the cork harden against the powder. When he withdrew the tamping rod he fit the squib into the hole the needle left, fit it all the way to the powder, and spooled the fuse out behind him as he crawled beyond the pillar at the mouth of his place.

"Fire," someone shouted from further down the seam. "Fire," the "i" drawn out and echoing through the mine, "fire in the hole." From the echo's hesitation with the words, he knew the voice belonged to one of the Poles who worked deep in the mine and lived in the shanties down Polack Hollow outside of Black Bear. He had to wait for the blast before he could shoot.

The blast came and echoed and the overburden of shale and limestone and sandstone rumbled above his head, the mountain whimpering to fall. He waited for the collapse that never came.

He pulled the tobacco and folded newspaper from the breast pocket of his shirt beneath the coveralls and ripped a thin strip from the page. He pressed the tobacco in and rolled the paper between his thumb and fingers to pack the cigarette tight. The newspaper tasted of salt and ink, and flecks of tobacco stuck to his tongue as he fitted the cigarette to his lip. He pulled the headlamp from his cap and lit the cigarette in the carbide flame.

The newspaper rested heavy on his lap. He told himself not to unfold the paper, not to let her see into his darkness, but he couldn't help himself. He unfolded the page and looked at the picture of her face he had drawn in heavy grease pencil across the newsprint. His first drawings of her had been so clear but each one had resembled her face less. This one looked almost nothing like her, the eyes too slanted and the mouth in a pose she never made. The hair was still hers and the cheekbones, but this picture could have been any woman but Karina. He folded the drawing on itself and stuffed the newspaper in his pocket.

"Fire," he yelled down the drift, his fingers cupped around one side of his mouth. "Fire. Fire in the hole." He touched his greasy cigarette to the fuse and leaned back against the pillar and waited for the world to be blown away.

*

COAL DUST IN THE CARBIDE FLAME, DIM MEMORIES SWIRL AND refract. Her breaths rattle and shake like overburden, her chest beats against the quilt, keeping time to her coughing. Blood on the flowered handkerchief.

He sets roof timbers. He hauls the tree trunks cut to length into the place and pulls them upright close to the ceiling and drives wooden wedges between the timbers and the shale roof, one hand on the rough timber, the other swinging the mallet. He can feel the press of splinters on his hand even through the leather gloves. Another light comes toward him through the dark and the dust. The light shimmies with footsteps and the footfalls echo down the drift as the body detached from the light moves closer. He pounds at the wedge with the mallet and waits for the body to pass.

The body turns the corner into his place. He cannot see the face of the squat man, but Ardieth knows from the hard hat the man wears that the body belongs to the straw boss and the straw boss never brings good news. Ardieth stoops and lifts another timber and points it toward the ceiling.

"Petty," the straw boss says. "She passed."

He had told her not to wash in the creek. "It's February, for Christ sake," he had told her. "This ain't San Juan. This ain't Ponce. This is West-by-God-Virginia, that creek is ice." She had answered in Spanish and he knew she did their wash in the creek anyway.

He crams the wedge between the timber and the roof and pounds the mallet against the wedge, pounds the mallet hard to drive that wedge deep and keep the world from collapsing.

"You hear me? Your wife. She's dead."

He cannot hear this, not from this man, this wimp of a man with his engineering degree and his manicured mustache, this man who never once felt a blister burst, never once pulled a half-ton cart to the drift mouth or laid the track the cart could roll on. He pounds the mallet against the wood even when the wedge will not go deeper.

"I heard you," he says.

He drops the mallet to the floor beside him and pulls off the gloves she made him buy. He steps out into the drift where the straw boss stands. He can rise to his full height here, no stooping to pound the mallet or crouching to swing the pick. He is more than a head taller than the straw boss but figures he gives up thirty pounds, all in the straw boss's gut.

"All right," the straw boss says. "She's down at the company store, in the basement. Already got her in the casket. We took the cost out of your credit at the store, so you're all squared away."

"No," he had told her again and again, "we can't afford new boots or gloves. I'll make with what I got. We're neck deep in debt as it is and the store won't give up no more credit. Every cent of credit comes out of my hide."

"We're all real sorry for your loss," the straw boss tells him. "Be back tomorrow at the whistle."

*

THE BATHHOUSE WAS POOLED WITH STEAM AND THE SMELL OF MEN. The lights suspended from the ceiling shone dim through the steam. He had never showered there until a few months ago. Only bachelors used the bathhouse for their Saturday wash, the company charging two cents a shower and the scrip hard to come by for any man, let alone a man with a wife to heat his Saturday bath in the big galvanized tub in their kitchen.

Steam stuck to his clothes and skin as he peeled away the sooted coveralls and sweaty long johns and hung them from a chain and cranked the chain toward the ceiling. The camp had no running water except in the bathhouse and the foreman's big house on the hill. Folks claimed the foreman's tub to be claw-footed in solid gold and Ardieth saw little reason to doubt word-of-mouth.

He entered the steam and pulled the chain on the flat faucet. The warm water fell out on his head in a trickle as he ran his fingers through his matted hair and scrubbed at his scalp with a bar of soap. The soap did little but grind the coal dust thicker into his hair. He rubbed both hands across his face to slough away the soot but he could never get the black dust from the folds of his eyelids. He could walk into a church in a strange town and spot a scrubbed-clean miner in his Sunday best from the coal dust mascara tattooed around his lashes.

A long body came through the steam toward him. He knew the body for Preacher from the skinny, bone-white fingers that stretched to his knees with his slouched gait. His name was John Scarborough but they all called him Preacher because he ran the Sunday service in the clapboard chapel and wrote Scripture on the fire boss's chalkboard every morning when he went into the mine to pick and blast and shovel his ten tons like every other man in camp. Preacher came right up to him, put his mouth near Ardieth's ear.

"Meeting," Preacher said. "New ground at midnight."

Word had passed along the camp that an agitator had come down from Charleston and been hired on without Justus Collins catching word. Ardieth had feared the night a meeting would be called. Then the decisions would be expected. He would have to choose.

"Right," he told Preacher. "You'll be there."

"I will. And so will you if you know what's good for this camp."

He yanked the chain and cut the water from the faucet. The steam and soap burned at his eyes. He had to show his loyalties to the company or to the men but he felt no loyalty to any of them. Damn the company and damn the men. Preacher was the only one he could care about. Preacher was the only one there with him in that hole in

February, the only one who dug and sweated through the cold night and lamplight as they carved that trench he never thought he would leave. Buried too, he had thought, may as well lie down in the dirt and frost.

"I don't know what's good for no one," he said. "But I'll be there."

*

"*VE Y ACUÉSTATE,*" SHE SAYS. THEN, IN HER BROKEN ENGLISH, "I HEAT water."

He lies on the scrubbed board floor and feels the hardness against his clenched muscles and watches the coal dust scatter across the boards she keeps so clean in the never-ending battle with the dust that coats everything in camp, the dust that wends its way through cracks in the walls and floors and drifts in through open doors and windows.

She wakes him by shaking his leg with her foot. "The water is hot," she tells him.

She pries the boots from his feet and sets them on the stoop behind their house then helps him peel off the coveralls and his long underwear. He steps into the galvanized tub and the water is hot to his calves. She helps him fold himself into the tub, his knees against his chest and his back against the cool metal lip.

She takes the bar of soap to his neck and shoulders and grinds the soot away. He loves the way she presses harder the farther down his back she goes, the way she treats him like a tub of laundry, the way she hums her laments as she works. She presses her lips to his neck while she rubs the soap along his spine. He feels his hardness grow against his thigh as she bites at his neck and runs her finger down the tip of his spine and along the crack of his ass. He reaches behind him and pinches her breast.

She bats away his hand. "You'll dirty my clean dress," she says.

*

IF HE STRETCHED HIS ARMS TO THEIR FULL LENGTH HE COULD touch the walls on either side of the shanty. He poured water into the ceramic basin and looked at his face in the small mirror suspended on a length of copper that rose upward from the back of the basin. A single oil lamp lighted the room and his face stood in shadow and reflection of the lamp on the table behind him. He wondered why he still shaved if no one would run her fingers across his face. Habit, he figured. Ritual. Or he was superstitious and felt her ghost at his side watching him, waiting for him to scrape away his workface with the straight razor he kept stropped to a thin point.

He would have felt her ghost more if he still lived in that Jenny Lind house by the railroad tracks, but the company had taken the house soon after he put her in the ground. Another family needed the house and the company owned it, so he couldn't stop them. We can put you up in one of our bachelor quarters, the straw boss had said. The company men never used the word "shanty," but all the miners knew that's what they were, a small room crammed with necessary furniture. Brass single bed, small table, caneback chair, the basin, and a coal burning stove that he could heat a pot or a kettle on but would have to fire up the furnace to do so. He took up the mole-hair brush and shook it against the soap in his mug and lathered his cheeks.

The edge of the razor pressed into the thin flesh above his Adam's apple as he held his soapy chin between his thumb and the knuckle of his forefinger. He pulled the blade up and stripped away the soap and the spiky hairs beneath the soap.

He had to sell off their furniture when he moved into the shanty. The company store gave him much less than he had bought the furniture for, barely enough credit to buy the few pieces in the shanty. He sold all her possessions to the camp wives, her dresses and combs and bows and the strange metal contraptions she used to curl her hair and eyelashes, or else he gave them away to the widows and daughters of dead miners, the women and girls cast off to fend for themselves in the tents and shanties at the edge of town when they no longer had men of use to the company.

He kept one trinket of Karina's, the small silver cross on a cheap chain that she brought with her from Puerto Rico, a dowry of sorts, and he hung the necklace from the corroded knob on the back of the unpainted door where it pinged against the wood every time he shut the door behind him. That sound of the cross against the door was the closest he came to her voice in his ear, or to the voice of God. He confused the cross for her ghost. Her ghost never spoke. Her ghost hung there always just out of his periphery, watching him without emotion or judgment. He was forgetting her face, and had long ago forgotten her voice and the smell of her smooth hips.

The water in the basin was cold as he splashed away the soap from his face. He had to wait until almost midnight before he could climb the mountain to the new ground and be among those who pledged their loyalties, if not their lives, to the Union. He considered boiling a pot of coffee but then the coal stove would heat the shanty to steaming and the walls were pressing in enough without the press of the furnace added to their weight. He splashed more cold water on his face and let it drip off him onto the splintered floorboards. He sat on the bed and waited for the moon to crest and the reckoning to come.

*

IN THE YELLOW LAMPLIGHT PREACHER LOOKS MORE A GHOST THAN he does in the daylight, the bright white flesh showing around the mud and clay caked to his long bone-thin fingers, the slight pink hue of his eyes now a glowing red like a crazed dog's. The hole reaches to Ardieth's chin. They keep stabbing the frozen earth with their spades and clubbing with mattocks as they churn away the clay and rock and soil.

Preacher stops and rests his hands against the handle of his mattock and leans his long weight against his hands. "I think that'll do," he says. "I think this is deep enough."

"A little deeper."

When they quit digging, the casket will have to be lowered into the hole and the hole filled in and then she will be gone. Ardieth will have to accept she is gone.

"We can dig a little deeper."

"Come, Ardie. It's near on dawn." Preacher tosses his mattock out of the hole then takes the spade away from Ardieth.

On either end of the trench are two lamps casting yellow light and shadow into the hole and to one side sits the wood casket. They climb out the other side and brush at the cold dirt clinging to their coveralls. They round the trench and approach the casket without passing words between them.

The company nailed the wooden lid to the rectangular box before he arrived, but the lid is fitted with a trap door sitting above her face. He pulls at the clasp on the door and lifts and stares down at the darkness around his wife's face. The moon isn't bright enough for him to see her laid there, only a gaping blackness that seems to stretch through the casket and into the earth and through the sandstone and limestone and shale to the seams of coal that undercut everything. He could lift one of the lamps and see down into that door, see that the casket stretches no further than the dirt on which it lies, but then he would see her face. The darkness tells him he doesn't want to see her face because then he will remember her exactly that way until the end of days. He drops the lid shut and the door cracks against the wooden casket.

"Do you want to say a few words?"

"I wouldn't know what to say."

"Do you want me to?"

"No."

They take up the ropes they had stretched under either end of the casket and crabwalk the wooden box to the trench and lower it in and begin to fill the hole.

*

ABOUT A DOZEN MEN WAITED IN A HALF-CIRCLE WHEN HE MADE his way to the new ground after tripping through the tree-speckled mountainside by the light of the full moon. He hadn't ventured to the new ground since Karina's death, had let their crops wither and decay and let other families take their staked-off space in the good soil. Now that the Union had come, a strike wouldn't be far behind. A strike meant no work, no pay, and no home, so the time would soon come when he would need to take up his spade and sow a spot in the new ground and replenish a store for when that strike came.

Even in the moonlight he made out Preacher in the crowd by his colorless hair and face that seemed to catch what little light the night sky provided and cast the glow back to the darkness around him. The same science that made the moon glow worked its charms on Preacher's pigmentless skin. Ardieth took the spot next to him.

"You just about missed the start. Wasn't sure you'd show."

"Which one's the agitator?"

"Organizer," Preacher said. He pointed to a wiry man with a bushy mustache who stood at the opposite end of the semicircle. "Name of Jenkins, I believe."

Ardieth had seen him in the mines and in the bathhouse, took him for any other miner, never suspected him of agitating. Jenkins laughed with someone who stood next to him, then stepped away from the semicircle and faced the men. All the conversations had been held in whispers but those murmurs ceased when Jenkins faced them.

"Y'all know who I am and who sent me and why I'm here," he said. "I'm here to deliver you from bondage and lead you to that promised land of fair wages and an honest workday that the UMW of A will guarantee you."

Jenkins sounded more like a man of God than an agitator, and Ardieth figured he could out preach Preacher four Sundays out of four. Jenkins pointed at him.

"You there. How much does Master Collins pay you for a ton of coal?"

Ardieth looked to both sides and hoped someone else would answer. No one did. "Twenty-five cent," he said.

"Twenty-five cent," Jenkins said. "Twenty-five cent a ton that you got to cut and blast and shovel and drag that loaded cart up to the mouth by yourself. That's the wage up and down Cabin Creek, boys. Cross the mountain, over at Paint Creek where they got their Union, where the UMW of A fights the coal bosses for them, them boys make thirty-five cent a ton. Up to the Kanawha Valley, where the Union is even stronger, they make forty-nine cent a ton. And in the

Central Competitive Field outside of West-by-God-Virginia, they make ninety cent. Ninety. But here you are, doing all the same work them boys is doing, and working longer days to do it, and y'all make twenty-five cent a ton."

Jenkins talked for nearly an hour and laid out all the evils of shoveling coal for Justus Collins, cribbage and dockage and unfair checkweighmen and the pay in scrip they could use only at the company store where all prices were inflated beyond anything at any store outside the camp. He promised the Union would take their complaints to Collins and force him to meet their demands if he wanted his coal dug out of the mountains. "Else he can go in that hole and dig it out himself," he said.

Ardieth was not sure the time was right to organize and strike, but Jenkins was convincing and he saw no way out. He would be seen as a coward if he left now, or worse, a spy, and he knew never to betray these men because he knew what these men were capable of when forced into a hole. So when the time came to sign the register and pay his dues and get his UMW of A card, he got in line with the other men. He took up the pencil and wrote his name on the list with the other names and the X's from those who couldn't read or write, put his money in Jenkins's hand, and stuffed the card in his pocket.

He knew he would be shot or there would be an accident in the mines if the bosses caught word of this meeting, and he knew there would be more meetings to come, more recruits to gather. He knew it was only a matter of time before the bosses knew everything.

*

THE MORNING BREEZE SUCKED THE PAPER CURTAINS AGAINST THE windowpanes in his shanty as he awoke. Even through the curtains, the shanty was lit up bright with the dawn. He lay in the small bed and remembered the way the sunlight lit up their house on those Sunday afternoons they would nap together and the way the breeze through the open windows pushed and pulled at the lace curtains. How quiet those afternoons were, quiet and still like the mines at night, but much brighter and warmer. The world seemed to have ended for their sake, to let them nap, let them make love. They would spend his one day a week off in their bed, their clothes bunched on the floorboards.

He pulled his pants from the hook by the door and slipped them around his legs. He left the suspenders hanging down around his knees. Her cross on the back of the door rattled against the wood. He put water on to boil for his coffee though he knew the shanty would soon bake with the heat of the stove where he burned the slag he collected off the steaming heaps and the scraps of coal blown off the open rail cars.

He sat at the metal-topped table and pulled the newspaper and tobacco toward him to roll a cigarette while he waited for the coffee to boil. He unfolded the sheet of newspaper. His drawing looked nothing like her, the smile and eyes all wrong. He couldn't remember her eyes but he knew these were not her eyes. Hers had been rounder, he thought, though he couldn't be certain.

The shanty smelled of sulfur as he struck a match to light his cigarette. He pressed the lit match to the drawing of her face, directly between the eyes, and watched the paper go up in greasy flame. Smoke plumed above the newsprint in his hand and he tried to augur the future, but he read nothing. He lit his cigarette in the flaming newsprint then cast the sheet into the coal stove.

He needed no augury to know his future. The bosses would learn of the Union and Jenkins the agitator would be lynched. The men who had joined would be blackballed. He would be among them, among the first to lose their jobs and their homes. More agitators would pour into the area, perhaps even old Mother Jones herself, and more men would join the cause. The water would be poured out and the strike would follow. They would be cast from their company homes and left to live in the wilderness. The Baldwin-Felts would come and there would be shots exchanged, bloodlettings between the mine-guard thugs and the unemployed and drunk miners. The fight would never end, no matter the victors.

Sometime before that, he would make his way up Cabin Creek to the tent colony where the widows and orphans, already cast out of their homes when their husbands and fathers lost their lives in the mines, lived in squalor. He would find a woman who had survived the winter and bring her home to be his wife. He would likely never love her, but he needed her, and her survival depended on him. Preacher would marry them in the clapboard chapel and they would move into one of the Jenny Linds by the tracks, away from the creek and the shanties and the outhouses.

The kettle whistled and he poured coffee into his only mug. When he sat back at the table, he pulled another sheet of newspaper toward him and flattened it out on the metal tabletop. The coffee tasted bitter and strong without milk to cut it. He took up the grease pencil and sketched thick lines across the newsprint. He tried to remember Karina's eyes but could not. The face took shape on the page but he knew it was not her face. For all he knew, it could well be the face of the woman he would marry, but it was certainly not the face of his wife. He had buried that face in the darkness and the dirt and would never remember her as she had been in life.

ACKNOWLEDGEMENTS

I WOULD LIKE TO THANK EVERYONE AT SOUTHEAST MISSOURI State University Press for making this book a reality, especially James Brubaker, Jenny Yang Cropp, Austin Neumeyer, and Savanna Halfhaker.

Thank you to all the publishers and journals where some of these stories originally appeared, some in different forms or with different titles: *Big Muddy* ("Dessert in the Dinner Hole"), *Failbetter* ("The Dog You Feed"), *Stickman Review* ("Donation"), and *The RS 500* ("Those Girls").

Thank you to everyone in the English Department at Oklahoma State University, where I wrote most of these stories as a graduate student. Special thanks to my teachers, Toni Graham and Jon Billman. Toni, this book would not exist if not for your guidance and the fires you lit and kept lit. Jon, you taught me more than you probably realize about writing and about life. I cannot thank the two of you enough. Thank you to Ron Brooks, Elizabeth Grubgeld, and Allen Finchum for reading the version of this book I submitted as a dissertation. Thank you to everyone in workshop who gave feedback on early drafts of some of these stories.

Thank you to all the teachers who taught me and shaped me as a writer, especially Aaron Gwyn and Alan Tinkler who set me on this path.

Thank you to all my colleagues in the Department of English at Coastal Carolina University for your support and encouragement as I finished writing and revising this book. Special shout out to Jeremy Griffin who gave me a nudge when I needed one.

The cover is a detail from a 1949 panoramic of the day shift at Stanaford Mine No. 1; that's my grandfather, Woodrow Gulf Scarborough, above the "k" in "Creek." Thank you to Jeff Rich for helping me scan it.

My family deserves the biggest thanks of all for their love and belief, especially my parents, Steve and Cathy Cross. Mom, you gave me the love of words that brought me here. Dad, you were the first storyteller I ever knew, and so many of these are really your stories in one way or another. Thank you to Caleb, Amely, Amelia, and Catalina. Thank you to all the Crosses, the Scarboroughs, the Pettys, the Fokkens, the Wrases, the Urbans, and the Sophers. I love you all.

But mostly, thank you to Jessica Fokken and Callum Fokken-Cross who make everything I do worth doing.